Lightning Strikes

Jan Irving adds her very own brand of humour and imagination to a tried and tested type of story, and, viola, you've got a book that will make you laugh while trying to recover from the very hot between-the-bedfurs activity that is liberally sprinkled throughout the pages… ~ *QMO Books*

Total-E-Bound Publishing books by Jan Irving:

Uncommon Cowboys Volume One
Straight Cowboy
Shifter Cowboy

Uncommon Cowboys Volume Two
Wounded Cowboy
A Plain, Ordinary Cowboy

Uncommon Cowboys
Shy Cowboy
A Cowboy in Ravenna

Power Games
The Wizard's Boy

Raw
His Landlady

Men of Station 57
Forbidden Fire

LIGHTNING STRIKES
Volume One

The Viking in my Bed

The Alien in my Kitchen

JAN IRVING

Lightning Strikes Volume One
ISBN # 978-0-85715-999-1

Interior text design by Claire Siemaszkiewicz
Total-E-Bound Publishing

Published in 2010 by Total-E-Bound Publishing, Think Tank, Ruston Way, Lincoln, LN6 7FL, United Kingdom.

Total-E-Bound Publishing is an imprint of Total-E-Ntwined Limited.

THE VIKING IN MY BED

Dedication

Be your own light—Buddha.
This one's for T.A. Chase.

Chapter One

Oh. That felt just toooo good.

Warm lips on my sweet spot. A lot of guys had made the mistake of thinking my sweet spot was in the obvious location, but I have a thing for having my right armpit licked and suckled, right over this little mole.

A soft beard scraped my skin with just the right amount of pressure. I shivered, arching my body.

I was aware I was close to waking up, like a boat about to bump onto a beach, but the hand stroking my bare chest felt so good I didn't want to. What was good about Thursday? Thursday was rain, midterms, coffee with Candy, and maybe I'd be able to squeeze in an hour boarding. Maybe.

Thursday was not vivid blue eyes staring into mine. A wide, delighted smile, like a kid's smile. Plump ribbons of braided blond hair that framed a tanned face. Miles of muscle that I was…stroking?

I sat up.

"Good. This will be better when you're awake, yes, *seiðmaðr*?" a heavily accented voice boomed.

He was so loud I covered my ears. The guy on top of me had a chest like a fog horn.

"What are you doing?" I squeaked.

I was naked. Since I'd moved into college residence, I could sleep naked, which saved a lot of time on laundry. My two other roommates were guys, so it's not like I was going to offend their tender sensibilities.

"I am making love to you, of course," the gigantic blond bellowed.

"Stop shouting!" I yelled.

He frowned, looking like a puzzled golden retriever. "*You* shouted."

"I live here!" I said with, I have to admit, very little logic. "Listen, Conan, can you get off me?"

He was built like Arnie and he was squishing my legs into my bed. This had to be a set up. I wondered who wanted to yank my, uh, tail—which was hard enough to wag right now.

But so was Conan's.

"I am not called Conan," he told me stiffly.

"Uh huh. So how much did my friends pay you?" He pushed back the blankets. His name might not be Conan, but if they made a rubber to fit his dick, it would be Conan-sized. I stared, my mouth watering.

Focus, I scolded myself. Just because he has the kind of cock I'd love to suck, I mean *love,* going down as far as I could on the monster and holding those big rocks and squeezing them…

Right, focus. I got out of bed and grabbed some briefs off the back of a chair.

Conan got out of bed and stood there, hands on his hips, as naked as Michelangelo's David.

"Where'd you put your clothes?" I looked around, then sniffed. "Do you smell smoke?"

"You ask a lot of questions," he noted.

"Is that a new kind of weed? What *is* that smell?" Had I left the boiler plate on again? Geez. It smelt like scorched earth in here. It hadn't been that long since I'd done the laundry.

"It is the mark of my passage to this world," Conan said.

Mark. I saw the hardwood floor was scuffed up. There was a burn on my fake wood wall and a seared heap of cloth that was a weird red colour. I stared at the wool, trying to figure out why it looked both familiar and strange. Oh, it had been dyed with raw madder. I'd helped Mom mix that natural dye for her weaving projects. I picked up the cloth, seeing fragments of a round neckline and cuffs with metal links featuring a snarling animal face. Wow. Mom would be really into this. I was about to ask Conan where he got the shirt when I noticed something else…

"Oh no, my graphic!" The new knot design I'd finished the night before was scorched, the paper curled. Damn. I stuffed it carefully in my messenger bag. Maybe I could photocopy the design. I wanted to show it to my prof later today.

I looked at the guy I'd woken up with.

He was very tall, towering over me. He wore a neatly trimmed dark blond beard. On either side of his face were golden braids, though the rest of his hair was long and free.

He was gorgeous, but obviously obsessed with some kind of role-playing. Figures there'd be something wrong with him since I'd woken up with him. I'd always picked the lemons in the barrel.

But he had a sweet smile.

And I had class in less than an hour.

I tossed more of my clothing, looking for a clean T-shirt. I found one with palm trees and camels my Mom had snagged for me on a trip to Cairo. It was clean. Now I needed my favourite pair of stonewashed jeans.

Conan was still standing there, glowering at me like I was a servant boy who'd forgotten to dress his royal highness.

"Okay," I said. "I gotta get to class. It was real funny." I swallowed. How he got me so hard, so excited. How he felt covering me. "Ha ha. Now go, your Lordship."

"I am Freyr Grímsson," he continued, in a language I didn't understand. Maybe it was Middle-earth. I found my jeans.

"There's coffee and, I think, some left over pizza in the fridge," I told him. "Bye."

I sneaked one last look at him over my shoulder as I snagged my backpack.

He took my breath away. Glowing golden skin, glowering at me out of electric-blue eyes, hands on his corded hips, the kind of hips with dimples created by muscles. He had scars on his body too. Probably some kind of makeup to go with his persona. His cock hung long from a thatch of blond hair almost as bright as the gold on his head. Holy geez. I gave it a wistful glance and then slammed the door behind me.

Haldir or Elderade, or whatever he called himself, bellowed again. I winced. Lucky my roommates were off on some kind of anthropological camping thing. Hopefully no one in the building would complain. Late night noise was tolerated. Early mornings, not so much.

"Bailey!" Candy was waiting for me. "We're going to be late!"

My best friend, Candy Drake, gave me a scandalised look out of large, soul-heavy brown eyes. Candy lived life as if she were a Regency romance heroine, with rules and etiquette. I'd had to get her drunk the night she'd got her first parking ticket. She was not a rebel at heart. Conformity was her thing.

Fortunately I understood her, since Candy and I had the same taste in reading. Growing up, we'd read all kinds. Candy's favourites were romantic suspense while mine were paranormal romances. We could spend hours talking about our favourite heroes.

"We won't be late. You have to factor in the time it takes for everyone to sit." I had it down to a science because I am not remotely a morning person. I just hit my stride by 2am.

Behind us, the door shook as if the mighty Thor had struck it with his hammer. Candy's mouth gaped. "Wow, did one of your roommates run out of coffee?"

Damn, there were actually splinters and a *hole* in my door!

"As if you don't know!" I flashed. I figured Candy had to be part of this. Today was my birthday. So she'd given me a Viking, like one of the demanding Alpha males in a Johanna Lindsey romance—except this guy took his role-playing a little too seriously.

Candy shoved back her long dark hair, her face so pale her freckles stood out like flecks of sawdust on cream. "Bailey!" she squeaked, much as I had earlier that morning.

She squeaked because the door exploded like a cannonball had fired through it.

And there he was, Gundar the Invincible, completely and magnificently naked except for his mighty sword, which had two crescent moon shapes on either side of a pommel, the metal beaten. Wow, it looked really authentic to my untrained eye. I was surprised he'd used it on my door when it must have set him back quite a bit of dough, a reproduction weapon like that.

He gave me an outraged look, as if I'd been the one to smash the freaking door.

All down the hallway of my residence, half-dressed students with blurry eyes and bed hair appeared. They poked their heads out, staring open-mouthed at Gundar the Destroyer's amazing ripped body.

"Bailey?" Candy gasped.

Gundar reached out one giant fist and snagged my T-shirt, dragging me to him.

"You will do your duty by me," he growled and shook me, like a puppy that had piddled on the rug.

"Stop!" Candy was hitting Gundar's free arm with her fists. His jewel-blue eyes widened and he glowered at me. "I have no wish to hurt your wench," he said.

I grabbed Candy's arms, not wanting my wench to get hurt either. "Candy, it's all right. He's, ah, mine," I said.

Gundar looked down at me with a half-smile.

"Yours?" Her eyes were accusing. "Bailey Moore, you have a new boyfriend and you didn't tell me?" She looked Thor over. "I want to know everything." Her voice had a sudden dreamy quality.

I blushed. "It's a joke!" I raised my voice for the other students. "My birthday. Ha ha."

I had two sudden epiphanies hit me. One, we were most definitely going to be late to class this morning. The second was that we couldn't stand in the hallway with half the building lusting over my Viking warrior. And, okay, a third one hit me. I needed coffee. Now.

"Come on." I tugged Gundar's arm. He didn't move, looking down at my grip on his tree trunk of an arm with something like amusement. It pissed me off. I wasn't built like Gundar, but I wasn't totally skinny. My arms had some definition from push ups.

"We will go," he announced in a gracious tone and allowed me to herd him and Candy through my beat-up door. Oh, man. How was I going to tell my roommates? I'd have to get it replaced pronto. Maybe we could swing by the recycled building supply store, where I could find a new one. That and some paint and I should be able to switch it out quick.

Which was going to eat up most of the day.

But first things first. Coffee.

"Oh no," Candy groaned as I got out the instant.

"Sorry, no Starbucks barista handy. You could always ask Thor here if he can make us coffee with the power of his magical sword," I said, slicing my Viking a look. He was pacing the room, sword thankfully lax at his side, studying the kitchen and couch area with some interest.

"I am not Thor," he boomed. "I have told you my name."

"I forgot it," I said.

He frowned thunderously. "You did not."

"Okay, I didn't." I looked at Candy who was sitting on my couch and watching my visitor. "It's Frey-er something."

"Freyr," my Viking supplied calmly. Then he pointed his broadsword at me, his fuck-up of a servant boy. "You will not forget."

I shook my head, reluctantly impressed. Frey certainly stayed in character.

"It smells like seriously burned toast in here," Candy said, wrinkling her nose.

"It must be the wiring in one of the walls," I said. "It smelt like that when I woke up."

"When you woke up with, um, Frey-ur," she said, running avid eyes over Frey's backside, which was on display as he bent down and picked up one of Jared's T-shirts. He studied it, even lifted it to his nose and sniffed.

"This does not smell of you," he told me, frowning.

"You can *smell* that?" I shook my head. For a second his reaction seemed so real… I was falling for his game. "Right, you have trained senses from hunting boar or whatever, right?"

"Yes," Frey said, as if he hadn't caught on I was being sarcastic. "I hunt."

I needed coffee. "Okay, water's boiled."

Candy reluctantly took a cup with instant milk whipped by my spoon, tons of sugar, cinnamon, coffee crystals and hot water. Her expression smoothed out after she tasted some. It sounds like junk, but I can make really good instant lattes.

"So what is going on?" she demanded, eyes half-slitted with pleasure.

Frey studied her, cocking his head. Then he gave me an imperious look.

"I'm already making you some," I grumbled. "Your Lordship."

He nodded firmly. "Yes."

I rolled my eyes before giving Candy the goods. "I woke up. He was in bed with me. End of story."

"You woke up with a Viking in your bed and you don't think that's a little strange?"

"Candy, it's my birthday."

"I know that!"

"So Jared, Miles… This has to be their doing. They hired Lord of the Rings here to give me a thrill." And what a thrill it had been with that warm mouth on my sweet spot and that hard body plastering me into the mattress. But I didn't have to share that with Candy. From the way she was looking at Frey, she'd probably figured it out.

Candy bit her lip as I finished making Frey's coffee. He didn't come and take the mug. I had to take it to him. Geez, he was annoying.

"But Bailey…" She put her mug down and got to her feet, hesitantly approaching Frey.

He took a sip of the coffee and then held it away from himself, looking shocked by the taste. Maybe he didn't think I could work such magic with instant.

"How do you explain this?" She was stroking his arm. I felt a rush of jealousy, which was stupid.

"Explain what?"

"These scars…" She looked up into Frey's eyes. "They're real."

Chapter Two

I took a closer look, of course. One shiny scar wrapped around his hip like a snake. It looked a bit like an appendix scar…except it was in the wrong place. "Uh." I scratched my chin.

"And there's one big one on his shoulder." Candy was behind our mysterious giant, hands tracing one mother of a puckered mark.

"Car accident?" I mused, feeling reluctant sympathy tighten my gut.

"Spear," Frey said, taking another meditative sip of his coffee. "This drink is most strange for *dagmál*, but pleasing."

"Spear?" I repeated. "Hokay, time for more coffee." I went back to making a mug for myself.

"That's it, that's all you have to say?" Candy gave me a disgusted look, hands on her hips.

"What do you want me to say?" I asked. "'Spear' is kind of a conversational non-starter, unless we're talking medieval jousting re-enactments." I gave Frey a look. "Which we probably are. Geez, looks like fake jousting is way more brutal than rugby."

"What if he's real?" Candy said in a very, very soft voice.

I slammed my mug down and strode to her, tugging her by the arm into the little hallway. "Don't say that," I hissed.

"Why not? Your place smells funky, he appears mysteriously and he's…cute but weird, like an alien. His hair is long and gorgeous, but it's seriously in need of conditioner and it looks like someone cut it with a knife. And those scars!"

"Wait, he's an ancient Viking who somehow popped into my room based on the fact he needs conditioner?" I widened my eyes at Candy and she flushed. "The only thing weird is *him.*" I jerked my head in Frey's direction. "He lacks any sense of perspective. He's not even a funny joke."

She screwed up her face at me, looking a bit like a pissed off Bichon, but because she was my best friend I refrained from mentioning that. "Well, I think he's funny," Candy said.

"Funny like the guy in an elevator who talks to imaginary ants."

"He hasn't done that!"

"He sliced and diced my door with a broadsword!"

"Well, it *is* your birthday," she said. "So this year, you got something truly unique."

We panted, nose to nose.

Then she wrinkled her face and grinned at me, that grin I hadn't been able to resist since the third grade when bullies had chased her home and I'd defended her. I'd got a bleeding lip and a black eye, but we'd been friends ever since.

"Truly unique I have," I sighed.

"Aw. Damn you, Bailey." She hugged me. "I'm sorry I didn't get you a cool Viking warrior. I got you Sherrilyn Kenyon's entire Dark Hunter series instead."

"Wow, really?" I could see myself losing some study time.

"I want more!" Frey bellowed, holding out his mug.

Gracious he was not.

"I know I'm going to regret this, but just what is *dagmál*?" I asked.

"It is the day meal," he said. "How is it you do not know this, guide?"

Right. I wondered which fantasy novel featured it. I sighed and poured my finished coffee into Frey's mug. Apparently he didn't get jittery from caffeine, possibly because he was already crazy.

"What am I going to do with you?" I asked him.

His blue eyes took on a certain gleam.

I cleared my throat.

Candy blushed again.

"Let me rephrase—how about some clothing?"

Frey looked down at his naked body and then back at me. He shrugged.

I had to agree. If you looked like him, why would you wear anything? Unfortunately, that would not get him safely out of my room. Somehow I felt responsible for the big lug. Maybe he was brain damaged from the same terrible car accident which had given him those odd scars. It was a theory I was warming up to.

What I didn't want was him flashing students and faculty and winding up in jail. That would not exactly put the candles on my birthday cake.

"So I take it your only clothing was that smouldering pile in my room?" How had he sneaked in here dressed like that in the first place? I mean, my birthday was nowhere close to Hallowe'en. Come to think of it, how had he got into my room? The outer door had still been locked when I'd left this morning and our windows were not accessible from the ground.

But thinking about how he'd got in here led to ideas that could make my ears bleed, so I left it. "You'll have to borrow some clothing."

"You are small," he pointed out.

"Not my clothes, Jared's. He's not quite as big as you are, but we'll have to make do."

"Why does he have to wear anything?" Candy asked.

"Not helping!" But I couldn't help but laugh. She wasn't my best friend for nothing. We had the same taste in men. And Frey was… I sighed, looking at all that tanned muscle we were going to cover up, those oak trunks for legs, that wide, defined chest. He definitely was the most amazing gift I'd ever received.

"I would speak with you," he said. "You are my guide in this world."

"I don't think so. Look, I'm missing class right now and I have a midterm at one." I was also pretty sure the kind of guide he needed wore a long white coat.

Frey and Candy followed me into Jared's jumble of a room. I noticed Candy looking around curiously. She had a thing for Jair she thought no one knew about, but I did. My roommate was hot, but I was protective of Candy. Jair had a lot of women on a string. I think Candy pictured Jared in the role of Mr Darcy, which was a fatal weakness.

As a young, gay man I'd learnt that the romance I found in books didn't exist in real life. It was better never to look for it.

I scrounged a purple tie-dye T-shirt with a vivid fuchsia heart in the centre, cannoning it to Frey.

Frey held the T-shirt up like it was a dead carcass. "I will not wear this."

"You'll wear it," I told him, looking around for pants and underwear that would fit him. I found some boxers with the solar system on them and some Malibu shorts. He could wear some of Jair's sandals on his massive feet.

"Wait, we have to condition his hair!" Candy said.

"I don't have time to give him the Queer Eye treatment. I have a midterm," I reminded her.

"I can style Frey-ur's hair while you take it."

"Frey," I corrected her. "It's easier."

"Frey," she repeated. "Yeah, that's easier than, um…whatever his name was."

"I will not wear this!" Frey thundered, shaking the tie-dye in one mighty fist. I was surprised the walls didn't crumble at the force of his rage.

I stepped into his space, hands on my hips. "Yeah, you will, because if you don't, you're going to wind up in jail."

"Jail is bad?"

I sighed. "Jail is very bad. I'm your guide, remember." I shoved the shirt against his broad chest with a satisfying thud. He looked pleased by this show of strength on my part, smiling approvingly. Apparently if I thumped him it was a turn on.

"You are my guide," he said. Then his wonderful thick, dark eyelashes lowered over his neon blue eyes. "I would enjoy my guide."

I rubbed my palms against my thighs, heart pounding.

He dropped the T-shirt and cupped my cheek before fitting his mouth confidently over mine.

I am an experienced kisser. I liked to stroke a guy with a curl of my tongue, setting in for a long, hot and heavy make out session. Thing is, most guys wanted to get on with it but I loved foreplay. I loved…someone's arms around me.

Frey pulled me against him, not subtle about how he wanted to hold me, wanted me in his arms. I was engulfed by his scent, which was leather and wood smoke. I forgot that my best friend was watching us and whimpered as he took my mouth.

His tongue penetrated me like a…hell, like a conquering Viking. The way he held me, I felt like a prize of war.

Frey lifted me so my feet left the ground. "*Seiðmaðr*," he whispered.

I wrapped my legs around his hips.

"Holy—" Candy gasped.

"*Shit!*" I smacked Frey's shoulders. He didn't stop nibbling my bottom lip, sucking it into his mouth. "Frey!"

Frey pulled back. He was breathing hard and his eyes were tightly closed. He shuddered as he lowered me to the ground.

"You are not unwilling to be my woman," he told me.

His woman? Abruptly I realised he meant the role in a more literal sense and my cheeks flamed. "Shut the fuck up!" I choked.

"Oh, I'd be willing," Candy said. "If Bailey doesn't want to be your woman, I mean."

I started pacing to try to work off the hard-on. I knew Candy was joking…wasn't she?

Candy watched me with wide eyes, as if she'd never seen me before, as if I'd suddenly surprised her by doing a magic trick or something. Perspiration dotted her forehead. "It's really hot in here," she said. I knew she really meant, *'You and your Viking were really hot when you kissed'.*

Yeah, it was hot in here. Steamy. "Go take care of his hair," I muttered.

"Huh?"

"You said you wanted to condition his hair."

"Oh!" She looked at Frey. "I'll take care of your hair."

Frey took her hand as if it was entirely natural someone would care for him like a servant.

When they disappeared into the bathroom I bent over Jared's desk, palms flat on the surface, my cock so hard and pulsing I thought I wouldn't be able to stand it.

Eventually the discomfort eased.

I heard splashing and laughter coming from the bathroom. I had to leave. Now. I had to go and study for this midterm. I was not going to let myself be charmed by the weirdo I'd woken up with this morning…

When I looked in the bathroom, Candy was cutting Frey's hair. I watched the scissors snip a long blade of damp blond hair, saw my giant's posture was hunched and anxious.

"It's all right," I said. "It doesn't look bad, it's down to the length of your shoulder blades."

"Guide," Frey said. He reached out and drew me closer with one of his big hands.

"Big baby," Candy muttered. "I give good haircuts."

"She does," I told Frey. "That's how she makes extra cash."

"I put a purple streak in Marla's hair yesterday," Candy said.

"Purple streak?" Frey repeated.

"Do you want one?"

"No," I answered for Frey. His hair was beautiful the way it was. "I'm your guide, right?"

"Yes."

"No purple streaks."

"Oh, all right!" Candy pouted.

"Stay," Frey ordered me. "I am hungry. I have not eaten since…" His eyes hazed, clouds over the blue. "There was a feast in my honour."

"Right, roasted boar and all that," I said.

His brow furrowed. "I do not remember. I am the guardian. I go where I am summoned to fight."

"Well, I don't remember what I ate for breakfast yesterday so it's no big deal if you can't remember this feast," I said, wanting to ease his sudden tension. His hand gripped mine tightly.

He looked at me, letting out a breath as Candy paused. His hair was now an even line, drying to a rich honey I wanted to tangle my fingers in. I'd done that this morning, while listening to the slow beat of his heart.

I dropped his hand.

"I have to go."

"No," Frey said, getting to his feet off the john.

"Hey, working here!" Candy huffed. "I haven't finished."

"I'm leaving."

"All right, quit freaking out," Candy said. "You always freak out when you like a guy, just waiting for him to stab you through the heart." She swallowed. "And when it happens I ask myself if it's because you expect it to happen, you know?"

"I'm not freaking out." I looked away. "Let go of my hand, Frey," I told him coldly. "Let go now."

He prowled to me, caged me by the sink with his arms. He was still naked, and his lusty armpit hair looked oddly primitive. I could see him easily in ancient dress. Maybe some kind of heavy circlet around his neck—what did they call those? A torque. And a cloak that rippled behind him like his hair.

"Guide," he said. "You must not forsake me."

I looked up into his eyes, feeling myself getting lost again.

"I have my life," I told him. "I have dinner with Mom whenever she's in town. Classes. Stuff." I ducked under his arm, closing the bathroom door behind me.

I heard him roar, heard something hit the bathroom floor, but by then I was in the hallway.

Chapter Three

"Huh?" I looked up into vivid blue eyes for the second time today. Misty from my nap, I smiled. "Pretty," I said.

The blue eyes widened. "So having a nap takes precedence over Celtic influences on modern society?" Professor Dunbar asked me in a sugary voice. "I am so pleased to hear that."

Shit. Those were not Frey's pretty blue eyes. Those were the frosty ones belonging to my professor, who kind of resembled a pissed-off Helen Mirren. I looked around the room, seeing it was deserted. I took the exam I'd been using as a pillow and handed it to her. I think I'd drooled on it.

"At least you didn't go over the time limit, since I'm pretty sure I heard you snoring for the past half hour," she noted dryly.

Professor Dunbar was one of the best teachers in our Seattle school. She had gone to Yale for her degrees and I enjoyed how she challenged me in a history class I hadn't initially been sure was going to do me much good, since I was more interested in graphic design.

She delved into magic and druids and shit. Very New Age compared to other teachers. She also taught a warrior yoga class that I took with my Mom when I had the time.

"Sorry! I, uh, got a strange start this morning."

Now she looked amused. "You're a student. You're supposed to have strange mornings."

"Yeah, pretty sure this one falls into the bizarre category," I said. I had a headache from sleeping so hard and then waking up again suddenly. I needed some caffeine. Frey had taken my fix. Thinking of Frey, my chest tightened.

"Are you all right?" she asked, sitting in the seat next to mine.

"Sure."

She studied me.

"I met this guy."

Her lips quirked. "Uh huh."

"I mean I met him in a kind of odd way."

"Online?"

"Nope. And anyway, online isn't an odd way to hook up anymore," I told her.

"It was in my day." More humour lit her eyes. "Yeah, yeah, that was ages ago." She'd gone to school with my Mom. "So what qualifies as odd?"

"He was in my bed when I woke up." I rubbed my palms against my desk. "He was just…there. I don't know how since the door was locked, the windows shut. I guess it was a really good gag, since it's my birthday."

"Hmmm." Her eyes went opaque behind her glasses.

"And there was this smell…and he has a shirt dyed with madder and a pitted metal sword."

She stiffened. An expression I couldn't read flashed across her face. "Was the smell like something burned?"

"I...yeah! How did you know that?"

"Remember I lent you those Celtic engravings as a reference, Bailey?" Now she looked stern. "You didn't by any chance...alter the designs for your art projects?"

"Sure I did." I had them in my messenger bag, so I dug them out, including the slightly burnt one. "I wanted to give them a twist, update them to the now, you know."

"I warned you *not* to do that," she said, then muttered, "but what were the chances you'd stumble on creating something with real power?" She ruffled through my art work. "Oh, my."

"What?" I was having trouble following her, especially after my unusual morning. Maybe my quota for weird was full. All I knew was I wanted to get back to Candy and check on Frey...and what was I going to do with him? He had to have a home, people, and yet he seemed so lost.

"This one." Sure enough, she tapped the burnt one I'd remade into a circle with ravens and eagles.

"I finished that one last night," I told her, pleased with it. It was the best one yet, a symbol I liked so much I was thinking of using it as a signature for my future work.

"It's the symbol for 'sanctuary'." She blew out a breath. "Holy green apples! Do you know what this can do?"

"Um."

"This is a powerful summoning, a door that you opened into this world!" Her eyes were very intense. I felt sweat break out on the back of my neck.

"I'll have to make some calls," she snapped, taking my piece and putting it into her briefcase. "That man from your bedroom, is he somewhere safe?"

"Yeah, he's with Candy. We're going to meet at the Bono Cafe for lattes." Anxiety was eating my heart. I didn't follow what Professor Dunbar was talking about but there was no doubt she was really alarmed.

By my artwork.

The day was just getting stranger.

"What you need to remember is things happen in *threes,*" she said. "Your man friend won't be the only thing that came through the door you opened."

I swallowed, my throat muscles working drily together. I snatched my messenger bag. "I'm going to the cafe," I said.

"Do that." She nodded. "I'll hold onto this power symbol. It can attract…things you'd never want to attract. It'll have to be disabled." She hurried off before I could ask her what she meant.

Could my graphic really somehow be connected to Frey showing up in my bed?

As I crossed the rose garden on campus, it started to rain again, so I decided to stop by residence for my woollen hoodie. My Mom had knitted it and it was a bit bright for my tastes, with hand-spun reds and fuchsias she'd picked up in Guatemala, but it was warm, and it looked like I'd need it today.

I looked up at the windows of my residence and saw a shadow move. Was Frey still there? My heartbeat picked up.

I reached the top of the stairs. My broken door made me remember I'd have to take care of it. I caught the smell—sweet and wet and rotting. Holy shit!

A pool of dark liquid seeped from under the battered door.

"Look, dude, I know it's your birthday, but we've all got midterms right now," Amber Beatty said. She was in the room next to the one I shared with my friends. "First your door gets wrecked by some berserker hottie and now this."

A damp puff of air that smelt like a dirty urinal lifted my hair through the open gaps in the door. I absolutely did not want to go in there.

"Anything happen while I was taking my midterm?"

Amber frowned at me. "My window shattered about fifteen minutes ago. Just…imploded. I opened my door and it stinks! You need to mop that shit up."

"I'll get right on that," I said, even though there was no way I was going into my room. I took out my BlackBerry and called Professor Dunbar's number. When I got her voicemail, I left her a message to call me back right away.

Things happen in threes.

"It might be a good idea if you finished up studying in the library," I told Amber. She nodded and I noticed other students leaving in a hurry. Apparently the smell—gah, it was fucking *awful*!—was enough to encourage people to leave.

It was pouring when I got back outside, but it was a hell of a lot better than the stench inside my building. I needed to get to Candy and Frey. I remembered Frey's face when he'd said I must not forsake him.

But I hadn't forsaken him, damn it. I just… I'd needed to get away from him and how focused he seemed on me. I couldn't be who he thought I was.

I caught the smell of burnt cookies, sharp in the cool, misty air. I was almost at the cafe, where they must be roasting coffee beans this afternoon. I dashed into the campus knot garden of ragged evergreen shrubs, dripping with heavy, cold drops that spattered against the back of my neck, soaking my hair to my skin.

Even though the cafe was close by, inside the walls of shrubbery I felt like Alice lost in another world. I tripped, my ankle giving way so I fell into a freshly dug hole in the ground. It was like something a golden retriever would dig in a backyard. "Fuck!"

The gully was brim full of icy water, the rain coming down too hard for it to be absorbed into the earth. Shuddering with chill, I tried to get to my feet, the mud slippery under my sneakers. Great, I was going to arrive for coffee looking like I'd done a round of mud wrestling.

I caught the smell first, that sweet, rotting scent that overlaid the clean, cool wetness. I choked on my own saliva, the stinky bathroom aroma making my eyes sting.

Something silvery flashed, scoring through my T-shirt to rip flesh. I screamed, my voice high and panicked. Blood dripped like pink, diluted tears from my wound. *This isn't happening.*

My attacker wasn't some kind of manic groundskeeper out to settle the score or a crazed student with a Japanese hand rake. It was… Red eyes, burning like the tips of hot pokers. A snarl exposing razor teeth in a pointed muzzle.

It smiled at me.

I fell on my ass, skittering away on my palms and feet, heart thudding like hail. I'd watched enough episodes of the *X-Files* as a kid to know I was doomed.

A heavy broadsword swung, connecting with the creature in a solid smack, like a batter hitting a home run. The thing screeched and tumbled into the greenery. I caught the flash of angry red eyes, a slash of teeth.

Frey, his garish, borrowed tie-dye soaked, his hair dripping into his grim face. "*Guide!*"

"I'm all right!" I croaked. I got off my ass and crouched next to him, scanning for the…whatever it was.

Frey lowered his sword. "It has gone from this place, though I fear it will return."

I grabbed his arm.

"It has gone, my guide." His voice was gentle as he helped me to my feet and then put an arm like an oak branch around my shoulders.

"Coffee," I croaked. Damn, I was dizzy. And I was never going to get my fix at this rate.

"Oh my goddess!" Candy screeched again. "I'm going to *vomit!*"

"Cut that out!" I growled at her. I had a hand clamped over my shoulder but fortunately, despite the greasy smear of blood on my fingers, the cuts were shallow. That didn't mean they didn't hurt—for some reason shallow cuts hurt like a bitch, like paper cuts.

Frey and I were standing in the entrance to Bono's, attracting a lot of attention from the afternoon coffee crowd. And Candy wasn't helping.

"But you're wounded. Oh. My. Goddess!"

"Believe me, I'm frickin' aware." I swayed and Frey took my arm again, guiding me into a chair. He knelt beside me like a knight about to pledge allegiance to his king. His sword rang against the concrete floor as he bowed his head.

"Frey?" I whispered.

When he didn't immediately respond, I looked at Candy. "A double caramel latte. Three shots of espresso."

"You're kidding. You need—"

"The uni hospital is next door. I'll go and get this looked at, but first I need..." I sighed, wincing as I settled into the leather club chair. "Coffee. This day started out bad because I didn't get much."

"Okay, coffee I can do." Her face hardened as she took a deep breath, like she was soldiering up.

When she was gone, I reached out to Frey, raking my hand through his cold soaking hair. "You saved me," I said, very softly.

"I am...shamed."

I lifted his face to better understand him. The subdued light highlighted the brutal lines of his cheekbones, the solemn look in his eyes. "Why shamed?"

"I did not protect you from the Shadow creature."

"I'm pretty sure you did." I shrugged, then winced. Shit. I had to remember not to shrug. Not for at least four centuries. "I mean... I'm here, aren't I? That thing—"

"It would have disembowelled you and buried you in its burrow."

"Lovely."

"It might also have taken a few choice organs and eaten them while they were warm and fresh," Frey added.

"I think it was in my room," I said. "My place had the same reek."

I couldn't deny that something was seriously off. First Frey, then my prof's spooky reaction to my graphic and then that thing that could not have been real. And yet it had been.

"It followed me to this place, this time," Frey said, his scarred, callused hands gripping his sword. "It is strange, usually it is the guide who summons me with a purpose, but you seemed unprepared for my arrival."

"Frey, I think we need to talk about where you come from." I swallowed. *And if I had anything to do with you being here now.*

Chapter Four

"I am a guardian," Frey said in the same tone he used when he referred to me as the guide. As if I should know this shit.

"Ah, yeah. Look, I'm not up on this guide stuff, so maybe you can explain what a guardian is exactly?"

Frey shook his head. "You do not need to understand. You are the guide, as I am the guardian." His eyelashes fell, but not before I caught a sizzling flash of blue. "The guardian and the guide fit together."

I swallowed. How could I suddenly be thinking of sex when out in the cold rain, in the shrubs next to Bono's, I'd nearly got shredded and eaten by a creature with jagged teeth and eyes that glowed like cherry-coloured Christmas bulbs?

But I was thinking of sex. One look, one touch from Frey and I was hard, ready to be his woman in the literal sense. Damn.

"Where are you from?" I took out a pad and paper. Sometimes when I write things down or draw them, they make more sense to me.

He said something that sounded like 'nor-reeg-eh'. I processed and then the light bulb switched on. "Norway," I said.

"Long time past," he continued.

"When you, ah, hunted boar and…" whatever Vikings did.

He nodded.

"But you're here. Somehow, you're here."

"I have been called three times." He frowned. "Different places, times. I feasted in victory and then… I slept. Until I was called once again, summoned by the guide." He nodded to me.

"Oh, shit." So my graphic art project had really somehow called him here? I scrubbed my jaw. "Frey, it was an accident."

He shook his head. "There are no accidents. The guide is never wrong."

"I—" I looked down at the empty page where I'd so far written the words 'Norway' and 'ancient'. "I had a school project due. Professor Dunbar lent me some old engravings. She warned me—" I swallowed. "I thought it was just some New Age shit. I wanted to get high marks." No, it wasn't just that, I admitted to myself. I'd wanted to outshine everyone. I'd wanted to show off. There was a cute guy in my art class and—

And now Frey was here and that thing, that wolverine-glowing-eyes thing was here and my door was trashed and I couldn't go back to my dorm room.

"The guide is never wrong."

"Oh, Christ."

"You are not yourself, guide." Frey put his sword through a loop in his belt. It should have looked ridiculous coupled with Malibu shorts and the tie-dye, but I remembered that sword slicing through the air, defending me. He sure as hell knew how to use it.

"Here's the coffee!" Candy called. She looked at my face. "Oh, you don't look so hot."

"The guide will drink of it," Frey said, making up my mind for me the same way I'd nixed him getting a purple streak.

Candy gave me the cup and I felt a buzz of vague annoyance that she went on autopilot when Frey told her to do something. I'd never managed that trick. She always argued with me.

Candy cocked her head as I blew on the coffee, taking in the feather mark worked into the steamed milk. I so had to try to replicate that with my instant. "Frey was very upset when you left."

I nodded, remembering the crashing sounds and bellowing when I'd left him with Candy and run away to class.

Nah, class was just an excuse. I'd just run. And Candy knew it.

"So we came to an understanding. He...wants to keep you safe. And he believes in you. FYI he's not one of those beautiful jerks you stalk until they give you what you expect and hurt you."

Now this was way too much revelation. I sucked in a breath to tell my well-meaning but out-of-line friend off.

"He's...sweet. That's all I'm sayin'." Candy stepped back and Frey lifted me in his powerful arms. It was totally Rhett Butler and why wasn't I yelling at him, yelling at them both?

But my shoulder was aching and I couldn't go back to my room and there was something out there, some *thing* that had tried to kill me.

"It's just a quick dash by the SUB building to general admissions," Candy was telling Frey. I opened my mouth to explain how the campus worked, but I yawned instead. And I didn't care that we had an audience, including a guy I'd done in a hallway a month ago. He was unshaven, all black leather and mirrored sunglasses, and who wears those things indoors on a rainy day?

In contrast, Frey was wood smoke, steady eyes and his body between me and danger.

I closed my eyes and almost fell asleep, despite the huge blue drops of cold rain that continued to fall.

After the scratches had been cleaned and bandaged, I tossed my shirt into the garbage. I didn't have anything to wear and I couldn't go back to my room, so I'd have to tough it out. When I walked out of the treatment room Frey looked me over and then immediately shed the tie-dye. For some reason that choked me up, probably because I was so fucking tired.

"Anything to get out of it, huh?" I said as I put it on. I was buried in it, of course, but it was warm from his body and hid the bandaged shoulder.

He smiled, all white, beautiful teeth. "It is colourful. I look better in chain mail, yes?"

"I don't know, do you?" I teased him.

"I needs must find some before our next battle."

"Oh." That took the wind out of my sails in a hurry. "There's, uh, going to be one?"

"Come, guide." His big hand on my shoulder should have made me want to defend my manhood. I was weaker than I thought.

Candy had her glasses on and her nose in a JR Ward book. She put the book back into her knapsack and looked me over critically.

"Five by five," I told her.

"Please." She rolled her eyes. "You look…fragile and shit."

"I always look that way." And I hated that like hell. "I have very translucent skin."

"So where are we going?" she asked.

"Ah…" A plan, I needed a plan. No, I needed about twelve hours of uninterrupted sleep and then more coffee. I woke to the fact I was stroking Frey's bare chest when Candy smirked. "I'm going to Mom's."

"Good idea," Candy said. "Is she home right now?"

I shook my head. My mom ran a natural dye and fair trade furniture store, so she wasn't home a lot. "Cambodia," I said. "So, uh…" I looked up into brilliant blue eyes. "We'll be all alone."

Frey smiled. "I would take you so that the whole settlement heard your cries of pleasure, *seiðmaðr.*"

I blushed and Candy grinned and waggled her eyebrows. Subtle she was not. But neither was Frey. Geez, I hope she wasn't going to ask to watch us together or something. She had a gleam in her eye now whenever Frey got friendly with me.

"Um, yeah, I think I could do without the 'whole settlement' knowing if we get busy."

"You are shy," he said.

"Frey…knock it off!" It was clearly a white flag. He roared with laughter. I'd never heard anyone actually do that, apart from books and evil villains in movies, but he did. I found myself smiling even as I led the way to my Smart car.

"Oops," Candy said, as Frey just stared at my car.

"I will ride," Frey said and then looked around for where I kept my noble steed.

"You're going to have to stuff yourself in the passenger side."

"I have seen automobiles on the vision box—"

"He means TV," Candy said.

"I figured."

"They have spacious leg room." Obviously he'd been sold on that advertising hook.

I sighed, rubbing my neck. "Frey, you're attracting attention with the bare chest and the long hair and—"

He looked around and smiled proudly and flexed his muscles when a girl and two guys walked by us, staring at my walking, talking, historical romance hero.

"I'm tired," I finished. "Get. In. The. Car."

He paled but set his jaw and I realised belatedly that he was afraid of my car. I opened my mouth to suggest we take a bus when Candy opened the passenger door. "I know it looks the size of a Campbell's soup can, but it gets great mileage and it's wicked good for the environment," she told Frey. "Come on, you get to be alone with Bailey. You know, in a house, all alone with a bed and his hidden stash of sex toys and everyth—"

"Thanks, Cand, I think he gets the picture," I snapped, blushing again.

Frey met my eyes and I saw uncertainty. "Trust me," I rasped. "I'm the guide."

"You are the guide," he repeated and taking a deep breath he folded his body to half its size and got into my car.

I waved at Candy. She took her phone out and tapped it and I nodded. Yeah, I'd call her when we were settled. But that wouldn't satisfy her. I saw her texting me and glanced quickly at my phone.

I want deets, boyfriend! She wanted to know what went down between me and Frey. Jesus. I wasn't far wrong in her wanting to watch us go at it. I wondered if she'd ask me to film it.

But my best friend had good taste in men.

I helped Frey fight into his seatbelt. I wanted him to put the sword in the back, but he wouldn't let it out of his reach. His insistence was a cold feather brushing my spine.

"Okay, ready?" I asked him.

Looking like he was manning up for combat he gave me an affirmative and we pulled out of the campus lot. Man, my palms were sweaty on the wheel. I was picking up on Frey's anxiety. I drove like I thought I'd lose my licence if I didn't keep perfectly aligned on my side of the street. Finally, I made myself relax.

Weirdly, when I did, Frey started enjoying himself. As we hit the little freeway that went through the mountain woods to the small town where Mom lived, he was looking around. I wondered again about this 'summoning' business. What kinds of times and places had he visited? And was it in a linear line, stretching back to his own time, and how had he got the job of a guardian?

I had lots of questions. I needed to sit down with my pad and paper and write them down so I could quiz Frey.

"Go faster?"

I smiled. "Yeah." I gave the car more gas and we roared down the road.

Frey threw his head back and gave a war cry.

When we pulled up at the house, Frey stayed frozen in the car.

Finally I got out and walked around to his side, wondering if he didn't know how to work the door. After a moment of him fiddling inside, it opened and he got out with a breath of relief. "Tight as the womb, yes?" he said.

"You're a big guy."

His eyes took on that gleam. "Very big," he said with pride. "As you will find out."

I rolled my eyes. "Someone loves themselves."

"That is never as satisfying."

I laughed. "That's a pretty good play on words, big guy." As I sobered, I just looked at him, his blond hair a little silver in the fading day, the two braids, the bright blue eyes, the warrior's tension. His chest was twice the size of mine, with tiny nipples puckered from the chill. "Come on, let's go inside."

But Frey paused, looking at the house. "Wood is good, yes?"

I grinned, thinking of the Beatles' song *Norwegian Wood.* "I know I like yours."

He laughed heartily at the joke on himself, but then nodded at the house. "Much wood."

"My dad was an architect," I told Frey. "He had that seventies 'back to nature' approach, so when he and Mom bought the cottage, we renovated it as a family. It's…a little different inside."

"I would meet the father of Bailey," he said.

"Uh…" Loss washed over me, fresh as if I were sixteen again. "He's gone. He passed away when I was a teenager."

"He was a teacher for you, a guide." It was a strange way to put it, but it fitted. It totally fitted.

"Yeah, he was. My Mom and I were both influenced by his belief in reuse, reinvention. That's why I have that car you aren't too fond of."

"You would have to have a good reason for such a steed," Frey said dryly.

I laughed again and unlocked the front door, ushering Frey into the house. "I know it smells a bit like a root cellar," I said. "Thing is, my Dad thought it would be a great idea to incorporate the raw granite bluff as a partial wall inside the house. Problem is when it rains, which it does a lot around here..." I nodded to the granite with rivulets of water running down. "This house kind of becomes a tribute to Frank Lloyd Wright's *Fallingwater*."

"This is a secure fortress," Frey said, placing a big palm against the rock wall. "Things cannot come at us from the earth itself."

"Oh, yeah..." I hadn't thought of that. And I could have gone a few more days without thinking of it. "That thing from campus, it could follow us here? We're going to see it again?"

"I cannot predict what is to come. Shadow creatures are the dogs of war, formidable. They killed the last guardian." He looked at me over his shoulder and I took in the scars on his body, the hand-hammered sword riding his hip, the grave blue eyes.

"How old are you?" I hit the switch for the electric fireplace in the great stone hearth which ran up like a tree trunk through the central part of the house. Immediately I caught that damp-wool scent that meant this place had been empty a while—which was good. I didn't want my Mom home while all this was going down.

Frey's eyes widened, as if he was surprised by the personal question. "I was ten and five when I became a guardian," he said.

"*Fifteen?* You were a..." I wasn't quite sure what a guardian was yet since I was slim on details of the job description, but I knew Frey didn't exactly play endless rounds of Monopoly. "Warrior at fifteen?"

"What else could I be, Bailey, son of—" He stopped.

"Fred," I said. "My Dad's name was Fred. But I'm just as much the son of my mother and she is Beth. Professor Dunbar would say a matrilineal line is equally legitimate."

"Bailey, son of Fred and Beth," he repeated, as if my name and my parent's names helped him fix my special place in the universe.

I moved closer to him, touched the shiny scar that ran down his right arm. "How old were you when this happened?"

He frowned at the mark, as if he had to think. Jesus, if I had a scar like that it would be a no brainer, which just showed how different we were. "I was ten and three. The settlement was attacked and I fought the raiders. Many were killed."

"Your family?"

He nodded.

"I'm sorry."

"It was a long time ago." There was the ghost of humour in his eyes. *This is my life.* He accepted it.

"Is that why you became a guardian, to, um, help other people?" I was still stroking his arm. I yanked my hand back, flushing, but he reached out, took it firmly, and replaced it on his skin. His silent message was clear, *touch me, I like it.*

Shit, I liked it too.

"It was not that simple," he sighed. Faint colour touched his cheeks. "I joined the raiders who destroyed my village."

"Oh." I didn't know what to say. It was clear Frey was expecting me to say something like 'how could you?' but my life…was cushy compared to what I knew of his. He'd been born in a time that was as alien to me as if he'd walked with dinosaurs.

"I was enslaved," he said. "It was…not good. Then I won my freedom with a sword. I was good at killing. I felt nothing."

"At fifteen…" It was hard to wrap my brain around it, but I guessed people didn't live very long back then and, at fifteen, he probably would have been tall, powerfully built. "How old are you now, do you know?"

"I am a guardian six cycles. I am ten and five and six." He frowned, as if counting took careful consideration.

"Twenty-one." Somehow I was leaning against him, my back against the chilly rock wall. He loomed over me. I reached up and touched his beard. "How are you still alive?"

"It is not magic," he told me as if he had had this conversation before. "It is the science of the druids. They understood the wheel of life, the stars and seasons. They battled the creatures who try to enter our world through a tear in space."

"The Shadow creatures!"

He nodded. "Guardians are drawn to a weakness in the fabric of space where a door is made."

"I made a door, I know, but it was a total accident."

"There are no accidents, guide," he chided. "I have said this."

"Yeah. So, you come through the door to fight monsters with the, uh, guide. What happens after you win?"

Frey smiled sadly. "We do not always win, Bailey, son of Fred and Beth."

The truth I'd been dancing around just spilled out. "I don't want you to get hurt!"

Frey lifted me. I wrapped my legs around his hips. I pulled him close, scrabbling hands on his broad back. He growled and kissed me, taking my mouth, his tongue hungry, stroking mine so I shuddered hard. Each stroke made my nipples pulse, made my erection ache. I was loose and slutty in his arms.

"You are ready to be taken as a woman," he whispered.

"Oh, yeah." Why deny it? I wanted him to fuck me. I got off thinking about it—my legs shoved apart, ankles over his massive shoulders so he could use me or maybe I'd be on top of a pillow on my bed and he'd be behind me, face tight as he took me…

"Where are your furs?"

"Furs?" My head had fallen back so he could run his teeth over my throat. I was ready to erupt, right here, right now. I wanted to cover him with my cum.

"Your sleeping place."

"My sleeping place is fur-free," I said, "except for Mable if she gets in my room. She's our Siamese cat."

"It is time to make you cry out as I pleasure you. No one in your village will have any doubt that I have made you a woman in my bed."

His ideas were a little archaic, but fuck it, the reality was a big '*yes*'! I had a feeling if he did me, I'd be willing to sing a few bars from *A Natural Woman*.

He gave my jeans an impatient tug. When he couldn't figure out how to unzip them, they gave with a primal ripping sound. He'd just torn my pants off!

"If I owned you, I would never permit you to wear clothing," he told me, moving me like a doll as he undressed me. "You would wear only my talisman."

"Not really politically correct," I said. His hand was on my cock. Oh, yeah, oh, God, I was going to cream just from his hand on me. "*Frey,*" I whimpered.

"I grow impatient." No kidding. He took me down to the sheepskin rug in front of the fireplace, shoving the tie-dye so it revealed my pointed nipples, which he tweaked. I cried out, getting into the idea of him owning me. He shoved the shreds of my jeans and boxers off so I lay naked, exposed...and a little vulnerable. Instinctively I raised a knee, not sure I was ready for—

He tore off his shorts. More ripping and then his monster-sized cock fell out, heavy and uncut and wet-tipped, ready for me.

But I was not ready for him. "Wait! We need... I need..."

His fingers pushed inside me.

"Ah!" I wasn't sure if that was pleasure or pain. I was frightened of him. I wanted him.

Chapter Five

Frey was feasting on my neck like he was a vampire who needed to feed, his hot tongue laving my skin. He pushed my arm up and put his mouth on my mole. My sweet spot.

I shouted.

My dick didn't care that Frey posed a clear and present danger to my heart. He might as well have been sucking my cock since the result was the same. He took his time, nuzzling my skin so I felt the silkiness of his beard, so he looked into my eyes, his so sober and blue, the eyes of a warrior who had grown up too fast in an alien world. That look lent solidity to the experience that wasn't anything like one of my light flirtations. This was a man who took what he wanted, but did not take the pleasure for granted. Because he might…die. And he knew it.

"Frey," I groaned.

"You are pleasured," he said.

Oh, yeah. He whispered his fingers along the sides of my neck and I felt them, callused, yet gentle on me. Those calluses came from handling that sword, just like the scars on his body emphasised he was a battle-hardened warrior.

And oh, geez. He was the perfect Johanna Lindsey hero.

Fantasy was meshing with reality.

"Wait."

"Your body does not want to pause, guide." He licked the side of my neck lavishly, so that I shivered with sensation. If he did that again, I'd come. I couldn't help myself.

"Have you…ah…made many men your, um, woman?"

Frey seemed more interested in sucking on my earlobe than answering my question.

"Frey!" I smacked his shoulder. That got his attention.

"You wish to hit me, to play the reluctant?" he asked, nodding as if we were playing a familiar game. "We can do that until I conquer you." His hands were on my thighs, splaying them open.

"Yikes, hang on." In another moment he'd mount me. Part of me wanted that, part of me shied away when the solid length of him glanced against my lower body. A spear indeed. "Didn't they use…olive oil or something in your day?"

"I would use my blood to come inside you." He lifted his sword to his wrist.

"Wait!" I gripped his arm before he could cut himself. "You can't do that! You can't *cut* yourself just to be with me." What the fuck? This was just sex. Didn't he get that? "You don't need to do that. I'm…" *Not worth it.*

"This guardian would die for his guide," Frey said. "What is a little pain?"

I swallowed. Whoa. That he would do it, make a wound just so he could have me. "You don't need to. I, uh, I have stuff."

"Stuff?"

"Remember how I made you that drink this morning? It's like that, something instant."

He nodded enthusiastically. "It was good. A man's drink."

I grinned at that. "Yeah, just don't say that to Candy."

He grunted. "To answer your question, guide, I am hungry for you." His expression turned grim. "In my last battle, I lost the guide."

Oh. So he'd lost someone he cared about? I sat up, pushing his irresistibleness to a safe distance. "This is too fast."

"I have told you we may yet fall."

"Okay, the 'tomorrow we die' thing may be a spur to your libido." I studied his lower body. "Not that you apparently need it. But it chills me out. We need food and I have questions, lots of them."

"You do indeed talk more than any guide before you," Frey said, with obvious disapproval. He pushed back hair out of his eyes, his tanned face setting them off like jewels.

"I guess people talk more in the twenty-first century."

"If you were a stable boy like my first guide, by now I would have bedded you. It would be most pleasing," Frey grumbled.

Thing is, I couldn't argue with him. He made my body sing.

"I can't get over the creepy feeling that thing is going to show up, attack me again," I told him.

Frey reached for his sword and his gaze went to the miles of windows that took in cedar and fir and granite.

"Hey, it's just a feeling!"

"You are the guide," he muttered.

I was getting sick of his reverence. It wasn't for me. He didn't know me.

I was on my feet, knowing I was going to fuck up large, but not caring. "Look, you want to know why you're really here?"

He just looked at me, bright blue eyes on my face, his own serious, like I was his king about to issue a decree. Jesus, he had no clue.

"You're here because I wanted to show off. There's a cute guy in my graphics class and I knew if I made up a cool Celtic logo I'd not only impress him, I'd also get a better grade than anyone else. *That* is why you are here."

"There are no accidents—"

"Bullshit!" I yelled at him. "And don't look at me like that anymore. Don't you get I'm not anything special? If you want a quick bang, fine. Ask around, you'll find out I never say no."

He was on his feet, getting his face in mine. "Do not insult the guide."

"I am the guide, so I know best!"

"You need to be soothed from your fears. You seem to have many, guide."

"Fuck you!"

He just looked at me. A rock would have had more to give.

I was getting nowhere.

I stomped up the spiral staircase to the second floor and the kitchen there. The first thing I noticed was I'd forgotten to water Mom's spider plants again so they hung limply over the rim of their pots. I grabbed the watering can and took care of them. Then I sat down at the simple wooden table and rubbed my eyes which were stinging because I was tired. I'd had a weird day. That was all it was.

Muscled arms wrapped around me from behind.

"What are you doing? I told you—"

"And I listened." He put my hand over the middle of his chest. "I heard you *here*."

Blue eyes burnt into my own. I felt naked, like he could see every time I'd let myself get fucked in bathroom stalls, in darkened corridors.

"I didn't used to be like this. I used to have self-respect," I told him. "I was waiting for someone special. What a joke, right?"

"You will respect yourself when we lie together in your furs," he told me smugly.

I laughed. "Oh, Jesus, Frey…"

He touched my chest, right over my heart. I felt it beat under his warm, broad palm. "There's no one like you," I whispered. "I'll never meet anyone like you again."

"I do not come from this time, this place," he said.

"No. And I guess… I guess once this thing is over, once you've done your guardian thing, you'll go, right? Poof, gone."

Frey was silent.

I shrugged. "No big."

"You say much that is not your heart." His palm pressed into my chest. "I will see to your comfort, guide."

"Look—" I was going to tell him I wasn't in the mood anymore, but he lifted the arm with the mole and pressed his mouth to my armpit again.

I moaned.

I pictured us with my eyes closed. I could see myself on the wooden kitchen chair where I'd eaten coco pops and done homework. My legs were open and he was kneeling between them, kissing the sensitive inside of my arm ardently, trailing the blue veins until he reached the inside of my elbow.

"Oh, God!"

Sparks seemed to rise from my skin with each brush of his beard against me, with the hot lash of his tongue. He ate me up, absorbing me with absolute attention.

He jerked me forwards and my eyes snapped open. His face was hard, his eyes closed as if touching me this way was painful for him. I felt like warm rain, falling all around him, encompassing him, and I wondered what it was like to sleep for hundreds of years. Did he dream? Did he ache to be touched?

"Yes!" he growled, as if he had read my thought. "Yes, I want to touch, smell, taste you. You have the power, little one."

"I'm not—"

"Argumentative." He took all the argument out of me when he opened my thighs wide and put them on his shoulders. He bent down and kissed the inside of my leg, as pale and vulnerable a place as the inside of my armpit.

I let out a scream.

"You are noisy as I pleasure you, it is good," Frey said. "I want to taste the issue of your body."

"Huh?" Then I got it. "Oh." I blushed. He wanted to suck me off and taste my cum. "Most guys wear condoms for that nowadays. Safety," I mumbled. Oh, geez. He was… His lips against my balls, plumped in one of his huge hands, hanging like fruit for him to suckle. And he did. Ravenously.

"I will keep you safe," Frey said. "It is my duty to excite you, to make you content to lie in my arms."

He took his duty frickin' seriously. My hands caged his skull as he suckled the tip of my cock, taking his time swallowing my respectable length. I tried to fuck his mouth, so eager, so on fire, like never before. Dream lover, he was my dream lover.

"Stay," he commanded me, holding my body so I couldn't do anything but quiver like a guitar string as he played me, over and over again, tuning me up so I was moaning continuously, shamelessly.

"Oh please, Frey!"

He laughed against my skin, the vibrations and the silky beard and the flash of white teeth and the devilish way he looked at me under heavy eyelids. He knew exactly how he worked me.

"Please… Please, Frey. I need it. I'm crazy for it."

"You are pleasured." He sounded smug again and I could tell from the smile on his shiny lips that he loved what he was doing, without reservation. There was no calculation there, that if he gave me X amount of oral, I'd return the favour, or twenty minutes of kissing time was enough before the main event.

Frey feasted on me.

Frey…cared.

My breath stalled and I heard nothing but my heart pounding in my chest as I stared at him. No. I couldn't fall for him. He had as much as admitted that once his mission was over, he'd leave.

The thought cut into my release, raw…hot…painful. I came, spurting on his lips and chin while he laughed in victory. I flew for him, shuddering, and Frey held onto me as if he'd never let me go.

I closed my eyes as he licked me, nuzzling around my sex for everything I'd given him. I tensed at the intimate contact so soon after climax. "Easy."

"You are young and strong. You can reach enjoyment again."

"Not now," I said, very softly. "Please." He could make me come again but if he did, I'd shatter.

"Guide." He lifted me, arranged me so I was sitting on him with my legs wrapped around his waist as he held me. I could feel him, huge and swollen, a little dangerous in his passion.

I was too enervated to do anything but lie limply in his arms, but he didn't seem to expect anything from me. He seemed to enjoy stroking my back, as aftershocks shook me. My climax had been that intense.

From the moment I'd woken up with him on top of me, my body had been heavy, waiting. Wanting to be crushed under him, to be conquered and forced to come.

He reached down and took my cock in his hand.

I felt utterly possessed in his grip, as if he owned my sexuality, as if he had me in a slave's collar from his time and whenever he wanted I would have to lie on my back and take his thrusts. He *owned* me.

And was that ever a hot thought. I felt myself harden in his hand and I whimpered. He smiled against my neck.

"Frey…"

The world tilted again. He lifted me so I hung over his back. "Hey!"

"Rope?" he prodded.

"Rope?" I echoed.

"This will do." He had one of the printed dishcloths my mom left out on the counter, and then he had another. He placed me back on the floor in front of the chair and then he tied my wrists above my head.

My heart was galloping, my cock so hard it speared wantonly into the air, flexing as he touched it with one casual finger.

I'd fantasised that I was his sex slave, but he was really making me into one and my body liked it.

He spread my legs wide so I was totally open and accessible for him and his hands lingered, stroking me, satisfaction firing the blue in his eyes. He liked me like this, liked me helpless and needy, my sex begging for his touch.

"You are not sad now," he said.

"It's like warrior yoga. Usually I'm so uncomfortable it's all I can think of, so I guess this is living in the present moment."

"I make you uncomfortable, guide?" His finger rimmed the tip of my cock, over and over again as I panted, my body trembling for him.

"I wanted you to take me the first time I saw you," I admitted. "I wanted you to tie me up and conquer me like a Viking."

"You were made for this, *seiðmaðr.*" He leant down and kissed me, his mouth wet and hot against mine, his beard rasping my skin. "You were made to be the pampered pet of a warrior."

His ideas were old-fashioned, but they sure as fuck were a turn on. I imagined myself back in his day, lying in his furs. The other warriors would know he pleasured me as I begged him to fuck me hard.

"I can see you tied up with leather straps, writhing on my bed, your lips parting as I feed you my manhood."

I could see that manhood, solid as an anvil. My mouth watered. It felt like forever since I'd craved the joy of sucking his cock. "Let me," I whispered. "I want to taste you too."

He stared at me with heavy eyes, his big chest rising and falling rapidly. "You want me to feed you as I fed on you?" he asked.

"Use me," I said. "I want to feel you take my mouth, I want to feel you push inside it, come down my throat."

"You are a slutty servant boy," he said. "But I find I like it."

He loomed over me, eyes intent as he reached down and prodded my mouth with his cock and I moaned.

Chapter Six

He felt strange in my mouth at first, large and alien, and I realised it was the shape of him. He was huge and uncut, not like any man I'd ever serviced. And the way he took over, his self-assurance had no trace of the politically correct.

I'd played around with a little spanking and Dominant/submissive stuff before, but Frey was firmly a square peg who had no interest in rounding his corners. If he wanted me tied up and helpless, if he wanted to take me, he would.

And God it made me hot to have him in my mouth, to have him thrust inside, judge just how deep he wanted to go. He held my head in his hands, looking down at me as I accommodated him, his blue eyes burning. He was getting off watching me.

I moaned and he hissed a guttural word, probably one I was better off not knowing, given his outlandish ideas about guy on guy. For Frey, there was the warrior and his boy. I really shouldn't love filling the boy role so much.

But I'd sooner turn down a really well made mocha.

Frey was dessert and I was more than ready to eat him.

Literally.

He shuddered and all that muscle, all that control, splintered as I took him as much as he claimed me. I'd always loved sucking a guy with a nice dick, but calling Frey's 'nice' was like calling a Botticelli 'pretty wallpaper'. I loved the thick veins, the springy bronze-blond hair, the way he groaned as he worked his hands on my skull, gentle, but needy.

He muttered things in his rough language, his head thrown back, his nipples hard points, his body shivering every time I licked and swallowed around him. I played him like the very fine instrument he was and God, I loved it, every moment of it. I could definitely live in the present moment—something my Mom preached as part of her yogic deal—if it meant losing myself in his musky scent, in the way his voice broke and he seemed to beg me to take all of him, to take him even deeper.

Tied up, body under his, I felt more powerful than I'd ever felt as I submitted to him, giving him free rein to fuck my mouth.

And he did.

He wasn't polite about it. He didn't apologise or look concerned like other guys.

He was not civilised.

He held me still and rutted, watching his cock slide in and out. He grunted, using me lustily. "You were made to do this, to have a cock in your mouth, *seiðmaðr,*" he muttered. His face was harsh. "I hope there will be many nights when I can tie you and take your mouth, listen to you as you pleasure me." His eyes narrowed. "Finish me."

Oh Jesus. The commanding tone, the warrior's barked order. I sucked strong and he shot into my mouth, spilled from it, dripping hot onto my chest.

That finished me. For the first time in my life, without a hand on my cock, I climaxed, coming like the eager, slutty boy he'd made me.

"Over and done," I said firmly.

Frey sat up, blinking at me, looking sleepy and satisfied. He'd untied my wrists and he pulled me close.

"Let me go." I shoved out of Frey's arms.

"Be at ease, guide."

"I'll be whatever the fuck I want," I told him. "The sex was great, but it's over. No snuggling."

Now the big lug actually looked hurt, broad forehead wrinkling like he didn't get me. "I am a desirable lover."

"I'm sure you're quite the medieval catch, but we need to eat and to talk. That thing is still out there."

"You have sensed it?" He stood, magnificently nude.

"How would I know?"

"You need food. You will be better tempered when all your appetites have been met." His eyes twinkled at me.

"Can you cook?" I lifted a brow.

"That is—"

"Let me guess, woman's work."

He gave me an innocent look.

"It's not cool for a guy not to be able to take care of himself." I lectured him the way my mom had lectured me when she'd insisted I learn to cook. "If you stay here long enough I'm going to at least show you how to brew your own coffee and use a microwave."

Since Frey wasn't concerned about dressing, I didn't put my stuff back on either. Instead, I dug out instant noodles and added water, putting two containers in the microwave while Frey watched, obviously entranced by modern cooking.

"The box has fire?" he asked as the light went on and the cups rotated.

"Yeah, on a molecular level."

He looked confused, so I stopped the microwave and took his broad hand, holding it over the warming food. His eyes widened when he felt the steam. "Truly this is a wonder."

"Dude, you travel through time and space." I pointed out. "That's the wonder."

But his delight was undiminished when I pulled out the cooked noodles, dumping his into a hand-thrown bowl to mix in the spice pack. "Mom would say you need some real veggies for fibre." I liked cooking for him. I couldn't take him holding me, but I could do a little cooking, keep it light.

I found some salad ingredients still in the crisper drawer. The lettuce was on the side of about-to-wilt, but it would do. I put it in the sink and let it soak up some cold water while I mixed the salad dressing from scratch.

"Never have I tasted such," Frey said, eyes tightly closed. He put the bowl to his lips and drank the last of the noodles. "The spice. So rare and costly. A gift."

"You can have mine too if you want," I said.

But he shook his head. "You must eat."

I mixed up the salad as he watched me. He didn't speak, but he studied my body as much as my face, making my blood heat.

"Salad." I put the plate in front of him and he cocked his head before cautiously taking his fork. I guessed eating salad was new to him.

"The salad dressing is on the dry side because I used red wine vinegar."

He attacked the salad, eating with the same focus he brought to fighting. "You made this with wine? A princely offering."

I flushed but damn, it was nice to hear his sincere appreciation. He drank the salad dressing after he'd eaten the greens. "You are a rare prize." He cupped my ass and I wondered how many tavern boys had got a friendly swat of approval from him in the past—followed by a lusty tumble.

"I'm something," I said. "And you're still hungry."

Frey looked abashed but despite all of his hulk, he was skinny, like a wolf in the dead of winter. Made sense if he spent so much time fighting or…sleeping between times until he was called up.

"Do you ever get to just…take a vacation?" I asked. "Lie on a beach?"

"I don't know what a vacation is. Many things are whispered to me as I rest that will help with the coming battle, but not that."

"It means take a break. Just lie around and eat, sleep…" *And make love*, but I didn't add that.

Frey shook his head. "Never in my life have I experienced such." Hesitantly he asked, "It is possible?"

"Yeah. I guess only kings in your day got free time."

"No, they did not." Frey sounded very certain.

"I'm going to put some water on to boil. I'll make you some pasta."

"I anticipate your next offering," he said, crossing muscled arms. "You are also a desirable bed partner with your great gift of cooking."

I flashed him a grin, but pointed to the drawer for pans. "Can you get me two pans, the big one and the smaller for sauce?"

He was hesitant, as if cooking were an esoteric art and he'd offend the gods if he made a mistake, but I coached him into setting the table while the water boiled.

"We need some fresh herbs. I'll go out to the greenhouse," I said.

Frey gripped my arm right away, tugging me so close to him I could feel his heart beating against my chest. My throat closed up and I was suddenly molten with lust. Geez, his blue, blue eyes staring down so sternly into mine…

"Where do you go?" One of the braids in his blond hair fell forward. I wanted to reach up and play with it.

I jerked my head towards the glass house beyond the patio. "Greenhouse. Mom insists on growing most of what she cooks. She could tell you all about the stuff they spray vegetables with, how it's much better to grow your own."

Frey still looked confused. "Spray?"

"Guess all they had in your day for fertiliser was manure."

"With the occasional saucy boy chopped up to improve the fields," he said.

I laughed, wanting to hug him. *Do not fall for this guy,* I reminded myself. *You can't keep him.*

"You will not leave the house."

"Excuse me?"

"Not without my body between you and what threatens," Frey said. He disappeared down the stairs and came back with his shorts and his sword. He should have looked ridiculous, but the scars on his body and the hard glint in his eye proclaimed him a seasoned warrior.

And he was willing to die. For me.

"Okay, we go together," I said.

He shook his head.

"Forget it, Frey. You're here because of my screw up. And I'm not letting you get killed because of it." I had to head downstairs to gather my clothes, shoving into them. Frey had left me the purple tie-dye T-shirt, but it wasn't hard to live with the flat, smooth planes of his muscled chest instead.

"You wish to go to the house of glass?"

I realised I'd been staring at him again and flushed. "Yeah." I felt stupid when we exited the kitchen, heading past wicker furniture that had moss growing on it since it had seen so many years. The flowers were gone, leggy leaves flattened to the planters. Everything was familiar but I felt a chilly feeling drag up my spine.

It was so quiet, not even the hush of the tree branches moving together in the breeze off the ocean.

Frey looked around sharply, his sword lifted.

I wanted to rush back to the house, lock the door, but this was my life. Despite the stinky apartment and the attack on campus, I couldn't spend it holed up in my house—and there was no guarantee I'd be safe anyway.

I opened the door, the creak loud and reassuring in the stillness. I blew out a breath of relief at this sign of normality. "Okay, I'll snip some basil and rosemary. Just take a sec." Warm water dripped from the ceiling onto my face. Damn, I should get by more often and open the windows in here. There was a lot of built-up condensation.

"Bailey!"

I whirled, saw Frey staring at me.

My hand came away from my cheek wet with fresh blood. I looked up. "Something's…bleeding?"

The thing exploded from a hanging basket stuffed with fanciful horn plants—brown feathers, claws, screaming as it went for me. It was huge in the small space, its shadow blocking the weak sunlight.

"A hawk!"

"It is infected; that is why it bleeds. You must leave this place!" Frey roared.

I grabbed the garden rake.

Blood drops, whooshing air. I fell back, seeing the bird's eyes, red and seeping as it raked the air above me. *"Jesus!"*

The hawk smashed itself against the glass wall, crazy to escape, again and again before it fell, giant wings mangled sticks.

I panted, "Still alive."

"It suffers." Frey knelt. He whispered something in his guttural tongue, reached out and touched the hawk.

It crumbled, dark wet ash.

A single bloody feather drifted to the greenhouse floor.

"What the fuck!"

Frey was on his feet again. He gripped my arm. "We return to the house now."

"Yeah, okay." I was leaning on him. Why was I doing that? I was fine. I wasn't hurt. "It attacked us. A wild bird. Why would it do that?"

He shoved me back in the kitchen, slammed the door behind us.

"And then you... It was ash. You touched it and—"

He dragged me to a chair.

"I don't...understand." My face felt stretched too tight and I was hot. My head echoed my drumming blood.

"Breathe." His hand was clamped around mine, squeezing. Remembering how he'd touched the hawk, I jerked mine back.

"You are pale."

Frey got my noodles, which I hadn't eaten. As I sat there, staring at him, he began to spoon them into my mouth. I ate. I didn't know what else to do.

After a while I tasted the spice he'd raved about. "You take the idea of comfort food to a whole new level," I said.

"You are yourself again." He put aside the food, cupped my cheek.

I squeezed my eyes shut. It was that or give in to the terrible urge to cry and I didn't do that. Not since Dad's funeral.

He pulled me close. "I will not let harm come to you."

"Fuck, I'm scared. I just can't find my footing. This is all too much. But I'm scared, Frey."

"I know."

"And I...don't want you to get hurt protecting me." The ball in my gut had been growing. His laughter, his adorable confusion, his beautiful blue eyes.

"It is a plan."

I was gripping his bare shoulders, my face pressed to his freshly cut hair. Oh, yeah, Candy had made use of the conditioner. It felt like silk.

"What?" I blinked, losing track for a moment. "What is a plan?"

"Candy says not getting hurt is a plan."

"Yeah," I sighed. "Just don't, okay?"

He brought me water in the same bowl he'd eaten noodles from. I drank it without bothering to tell him where the glasses were and then sagged back in the chair.

"You are recovered, guide?"

"Not hardly, but I need to know what the hell just happened. That bird..."

"It is the second part of the darkness that comes through the door you opened," Frey said. "You were attacked by the Skirmisher first. This was the work of the Whisperer."

"The hawk was some kind of monster?"

"It was infected by the energy of the Whisperer. It used the bird to attack us."

"Okay." I nodded. I'd seen enough horror movies for this to make a weird kind of sense. "My prof said things come in threes. You, the wolverine thing with the glowing eyes and now this Whisperer."

"Yes," Frey said. "Two of us, two of them."

"Dandy."

"You are pale again."

"When you touched it, it fell to ash."

"A small ability." Frey lifted his left hand. "I will not be able to make use of that gift for a day and a night, but I had to cleanse the bird of the infection or it might have spread."

"To what?"

"To you, guide. That is what it sought, to overcome you, to share its blood with yours and make you part of the darkness and the hunger."

Chapter Seven

My phone rang.

Frey snatched for his sword.

"Wait!" I didn't need him smashing my BlackBerry. "It's mine."

I followed the theme from *Star Wars* back down to the lower level. I saw the caller ID with relief. "Professor Dunbar, I left you a message."

"I was deep in research, Bailey." Her voice was reassuringly dry. "I do that sometimes. It's part of being a professor."

"Yeah, look, I need to talk to you." I looked at my Viking bodyguard glaring at me. "Uh, we do, I mean."

"Do you mean your special visitor?"

"We've…had some trippy experiences." My throat closed and my heart sped up. Frey reached out and touched my shoulder.

"Do you remember where my townhouse complex is?"

"You bet." It would be okay, I told myself, willing my heart to just goddamn stop pounding so hard. It was going to be okay. We'd go see her and she'd have information. She'd tell me what to do.

I retraced my steps and turned off the stove. "No time for pasta." But Frey looked a little forlorn so I made him a giant peanut butter and honey sandwich—local unpasteurised honey of course. "Did you know honeybees pollinate most of our food? They are under pressure from all the pesticides used so we're in danger of losing them," I said.

"What *is* this?" Frey's eyes were closed and he had an orgasmic look on his face.

"Peanut butter." I snagged my wallet and keys. "Food for the gods, right?"

"Right," Frey said.

Frey was every bit as reluctant the second time to get in my Smart car, but I gave him a stern look. He sulked once we were in motion, and I had to admit his hulking body was squished like his sandwich.

"You called me the guide," I said. "But see, you're wrong. Professor Dunbar is the one who really knows what's going on. She can help us. She knows about the Celtic symbol I messed with so she'll totally fix this."

"She is a druid?" Frey asked. "A wizard of your time?"

"Um, no. She's a professor at my school."

"But you are the guide," Frey said, predictably now.

"Yeah, yeah," I muttered, taking a right and heading out to the little island that was home to a few town homes built back in the seventies. Pretty good life, living on a beach, the cedar homes bleached like driftwood.

I parked on the street and took a deep breath. My hands didn't want to leave the steering wheel.

"Okay, let's go see her." I opened the door, feeling exposed.

The ground squished under our feet as we walked past wilted planters.

"I know she can help us," I told Frey. "If I'd listened to her…well, you and me would never have woken up together."

"That would be disappointing," Frey said.

When we got to the door, I knocked and we waited. I was aware of the soft sounds of the ocean, smooth as a lake and the faint hush of salt air. The cedar tree beside Professor Dunbar's house creaked as it shifted in the breeze.

I knocked again, beginning to tense up. "She's probably on the phone."

When she still didn't appear, I tried the knob and the door swung open. Inside was dark.

Frey hefted his sword. "Behind me," he ordered and his breath was visible in the dim light. A chill had breathed out from the open door, like the frozen breath of a dragon.

"But I just talked to her—" My mouth had dried up. I had the same freaky feeling I'd had back at my dorm, like it was the last place I wanted to enter. "She was fine. She's expecting us."

Frey entered and damn, if he was going in, I had to and I didn't want to. I wanted to go home to Mom's and lie on my bed and read a paperback romance, haze out the past day. I reached out and flipped a switch by the door. Nothing. The hallway light didn't come on.

"Professor Dunbar?" I called. I reached out and gripped Frey's arm. "Wait."

"I cannot."

"No, we'll go in but we need something first." I sprinted back to the car and opened it, grabbed a flashlight from the glove compartment. When I switched it on, Frey looked briefly disconcerted at the beam of light.

"It's too dark to go in without it."

Frey nodded. "The guide provides the way."

I grimaced, but yeah, I guess you could look at it that way. Not that a flashlight made me Merlin.

Frey went in first, sword raised, while I shone the light into the hallway. The powder room door was closed. I tried it, flipped the switch…and nothing. It looked like the power was out. I could see dim lights through the gathering mist outside other town houses, so it looked like only Professor Dunbar's was affected.

"Clear," I said, shutting the door behind me.

"Clear?" Frey asked, forehead wrinkled.

"Yeah, it's what cops say when they sweep a room and don't find anything."

Frey still looked confused but he lifted a shoulder as if to say, *who can understand this strange guide of mine?*

"Remind me to watch some TV with you soon. It'll be nice and numbifying." A tapping sound came from the kitchen. Tap-tap…pause. Tap-tap-tap. I didn't want to go in there, but Frey made that decision for us, pushing open the swinging door.

I spotted her laptop on the kitchen table, screen open and lit up. Something sizzled from a frying pan on the stove. "Dry. She burned whatever it is dry." I switched off the oven, seriously creeped out by the silent house. "What *is* that sound?"

Something warm and wet hit my face and I screeched, dropping the flashlight. Frey gave a battle cry and I heard the swing of his sword. The flashlight rolled back and forth, throwing light, moving shadow.

Throwing light in an arc over the palm of my left hand.

"Wait!" I yelled. "Hang on…" I was kneeling on the kitchen floor. My body had just taken over, decided to get me out of range of flying claws or whatever came next. "It's water. It's just water, not blood. The floor is soaked here."

Frey picked up the flashlight warily and then handed it to me as if afraid he'd disrupt its magic. It dripped in my hand, but I shone the beam around the kitchen. "Not coming from the sink." I raised the light, shot it to the ceiling. "Coming from the second floor. You can see it seeping from the corner."

I wiped my upper lip where sweat prickled. "I guess we better…go up there, check it out."

Frey was already striding through the kitchen, shoving the door open and heading for carpeted stairs that went to the second level of Professor Dunbar's town house. I'd come here a couple of times with my Mom, but I'd never gone upstairs.

It was concern for him that made me keep moving. I couldn't leave him alone. I couldn't shake the feeling that if I ever did that, he'd fall.

Plus I was worried about my teacher. She might be sarcastic and cynical, but that just made her my type of person. I was sure Candy would be just like her in twenty years.

"Frey, slow down!" I called when his broad back went out of range of my light. "I'm the fucking guide," I muttered.

"I heard you, guide." His voice teased me. Here in this awful waiting place of dripping water and icy temperatures.

When I reached the top of the stairs he was waiting for me, but he had his back to the wall, his sword lifted.

"The water has to be coming from a bathroom." I looked down the narrow hallway which had Persian runners and framed ethnic art. Like my Mom, the professor often travelled and liked to collect stuff.

All the doors were closed. Of course. Frey shoved the first one open and I opened the second one. Looked like her home office. A desktop was humming and a cup of coffee still had steam curling from it. I saw her BlackBerry sitting on the desk, as if that was where she'd left it after talking to me just a short time ago.

"One more door. Has to be the bathroom."

Frey turned the knob and water gushed out, pink water, like my Mom's favourite cochineal dye bath. But not only water. Professor Dunbar screeched, hands lifted like weapons, blood-red eyes streaming.

She took Frey down, gnawing horribly at his neck as if she wanted to rip the flesh from his jugular and then feast on it.

She and Frey rolled, smashing a hall table into kindling, while she gave another horrible sound of thwarted hunger.

"Be…ware, guide," Frey croaked. He hit her with his elbow. Her head snapped back but she barely seemed to feel the blow.

I snatched a lamp, yanking it free of its plug, running after them. They were fighting at the top of the stairs now and I caught the click of Professor's teeth as she tried to bite Frey again.

"Dead. Dead. Dead," she muttered.

Frey's head made contact with the next stair down. He gasped, eyes squeezed shut.

I brought the lamp down on Professor Dunbar's legs and she turned on me, smiling while those weeping pupil-less eyes held mine. "Naughty."

Frey grabbed her, fighting to subdue her. The muscles in Frey's arms strained. "Salt," he muttered. "Bailey!"

I couldn't get past them to the kitchen. I ran back to the bathroom, hoping Professor Dunbar was into the same things as Mom…and found muscle-relaxing sea salt in a tin by the tub. I didn't stop to shut off the overflowing water but squeaked down the hall in my soaking shoes.

She had Frey completely under her now and blood dripped from her eyes onto his skin. I opened the tin and tossed bath salts into her face.

She screamed as steam rose and her skin melted.

"Hate, hate!" she snarled at me.

I tossed more salt at her, driving her from Frey. "Bailey…leave now," he croaked.

"Oh hell no," I said. I glared at the thing that had been my teacher and a friend of the family. "Want more seasoning or are you done?"

She hissed at me and then slithered down the stairs, crawling backwards with her eyes on me. She disappeared from sight and a second later I heard the front door crash open.

Frey sat up, retrieved his sword. I dropped the flashlight and put my arm around him. His heart was pounding as hard as mine. He was bruised, one eye swelling, his mouth bloody. Scratch and bite marks peppered his chest and neck. "God, Frey," I whispered. "Oh, God."

His lips were a pale line. He closed his eyes, sucking in breath.

"What can I do to help?" I touched his cheek.

"You are unharmed?"

"Yeah, you took the brunt of it."

He nodded, as if that was fitting.

"Stupid bastard."

His eyes shot open. "I am not a bastard."

"Uh, right. Sorry, I didn't mean it literally." He was prickly over all kinds of weird shit that was meaningless in today's world. Probably it was just as well he wasn't staying. He'd be the Mork to my Mindy at any campus party I brought him to.

"We cannot..." I helped him get to his feet and he swayed. "Be sure she has left this place."

"Right." I helped him lean against the wall. He gripped his sword, his gaze on the stairs. "I'm going to turn the water off. And then...I guess we better, like, investigate. Try to find out what went down between Professor Dunbar being fine and dandy and turning red-eyed cannibal."

"It is a plan."

I kissed his shoulder and his eyes widened. "Why did you do that?" he asked.

"No reason," I mumbled, heading off to the bathroom. I shut off the taps in the sink, grimacing at the icy water. There were a few pink splotches, still looking like dye residue.

When I didn't immediately return, Frey appeared in the bathroom door.

"What happened to her, Frey? She's a monster."

"She was infected," Frey said. "She is a pawn of the Whisperer now. It reaches for the buried darkness inside, twists it with fear."

The miasma of a spiritual car wreck clung to the little room.

"Can we get her back?"

"I have never succeeded." He reached out, pushed the hair out of my eyes. "But for you, we can try, Bailey."

"I like it when you call me by my name," I said. "Not just guide." I felt like a boat that had been safely moored, but now I was cast adrift, rocking away from all signs of home. "She was going to tell me how to fix this. She knew stuff."

"Her knowledge remains stored in this house?"

I nodded. "Yeah. Maybe we can get some ideas off her computer. Wait!" I left the bathroom, feeling a spurt of energy despite the bruises and the heavy feeling in my heart. "She took the Celtic symbol I made. She said it had to be neutralised or something. Do you think that's why she's infected?"

"I don't sense the door here, not like when I came through it to your bedroom," Frey said. "And if she knew what it was, she would have taken steps to shield herself."

I looked out the window at a little garden pavillion on the rocks.

"Maybe she put it there, close at hand but not close enough to pose a danger to her. Why do we need it, anyway?"

"It is the way we send the creatures not of this world back to the void," Frey said. "And also, it is the door that will take me back to where I sleep."

"Oh." And suddenly I hoped we wouldn't find it.

Chapter Eight

"Oddly, I don't feel like goin' out there right at the moment." As I watched from the window, fog swirled in from the sea, covering the little garden pavillion so it became as elusive as the island of Avalon.

"The mist is unnatural. The creature waits for us," Frey said.

When he put his arm around me, I was conscious of how cold my feet were, how tired I felt. All this shit had happened in such a short span of time. One day I'd worried about when I'd get time to wash my accumulated dirty socks and cram for finals, the next…

"You are weary, guide."

"I'm not the one who's hurt." I pointed out.

He raised one eyebrow.

"Wait!" I swung around in his arms, touching his face, his upper chest. "That scratch that ran over your neck. The bite mark…"

"Gone, yes," he said. "It is another small talent, the healing, but like the other I will not be able to manifest it for a day and a night." His eyelids fell heavy over his blue eyes. "And I need a brief time to recover my energy."

I felt abruptly protective. Frey was still a mystery to me with his hidden talents married with his vulnerability. He was also slumped against his sword. My Viking was about ready to keel over.

"You need your long boat in a hurry."

He blinked. "Oh. This is humour?"

"Apparently not. There's a couch in the prof's home office," I said. "Let's secure the house and then you can rest there while I check through her notes, see if I can find something to help us."

Frey's face was like whitened bone under moonlight. Sweat sheened his forehead. He nodded and slumped at the top of the stairs as I went down and locked the front door, checked the back. I put down some towels in the kitchen, mopped up. I brought more up with me to the bathroom upstairs and took off my socks and shoes, leaving them to dry out while I cleaned up the bathroom.

"If we reconstruct from the hot pan in the kitchen and the still-steaming coffee in her office, she was cooking dinner and having coffee up here while she went through her notes. She'd probably just got off the phone with me when the, uh, Whisperer came calling."

Frey was on the couch now, arms around his knees. He'd stripped out of this clothing again, his beautiful body muscled and distracting with all those yards of silky skin. I wanted to kiss the tiny wisp of white blond hair between his nipples. He nodded, eyes almost closed as he watched me. He looked as if I'd worn him out after a bout of vigorous lovemaking, and how weird, that I'd use that word in my head.

'Lovemaking'. It wasn't something I had any experience of, except in the books I read.

"I guess the healing thing really drains you, huh?"

Frey nodded. "It could have been worse, but the poisoned blood touched my skin."

Touched his skin, because he'd made damn sure it hadn't touched *mine*.

"Thanks," I said.

"I need no thanks."

"I disagree." I cleared my throat. "I'm going to see what I can find out from her notes. She used some kind of shorthand I'm not sure I can decipher, but she left her files open, so I may score there."

"I trust you."

He trusted me, Bailey, not the guide. It gave me a glow, even when I looked over my shoulder and saw he'd fallen asleep. His sword was beside the couch, there if he needed it, but he was out like a light.

It was good not to be alone as the fog hugged Professor Dunbar's town house like felting wool, snug and stifling. A dog snarled just beyond that soup, and I wondered if it had been infected. Would it attack Frey and me if we tried to leave the house?

And okay, that cheery thought wasn't getting me anywhere.

I'd been relying on Professor Dunbar to give me the answers, to get me off the hook. Now I'd have to rely on myself. I might have sloppy housemate skills, I might sleep through first classes in the morning, but I had top grades. I should be able to figure this out.

If I didn't, Frey could get hurt again.

I looked at him, saw he'd curled into the foetal position. His skin was pebbled from the chill encompassing the house. I got up, found a hand-crocheted afghan and tucked it over him. His long hair was wrapped around his forehead, tumbled under one cheek. It was warm from his body when I touched it.

I grunted in disgust at myself. I was dithering because I was insecure. I wasn't sure I would find anything.

The professor's notes were awash. As I'd told Frey, she'd used some kind of shorthand I couldn't read, but when I scanned the entry she'd been writing on her computer, I discovered it was a kind of journal. She used shorthand there too, but this I could follow.

B couldn't be trusted not to fool around with the symbol I gave him, but I'd anticipated that, of course. He has the arrogance of the young. He had no idea that the door existed, or that because he is a natural guide, he is the only one who can open or close it.

Now I have what I want. The three are here, and I can use them to solve my little problem of being stuck in a rut. I deserved that promotion, not that fool they passed me over for.

The guardian won't be a problem. From what B said, the Viking is focused on him, needs to protect him. I can use that.

Soon I'll have exactly what I want.

I had to read it twice. It was like she'd reached through the screen and slapped me. I was young, arrogant…and easily manipulated.

She'd planned this, wanted me to fool around with that symbol from the beginning.

She'd wanted me to open the door.

"Guide," Frey called softly. "Bailey, I can sense your distress."

I looked at him. I didn't know what to say. I'd thought it was bad that I'd done this by accident, but knowing I'd been used, that I'd just been a tool…

"She wanted you here," I told Frey. "She wanted me to open the door."

Frey sat up, offered me a broad, scarred hand. "I wondered."

I stared at him.

"Bailey, you are…gentle. You do not expect this kind of betrayal."

"You mean I'm an idiot."

He tugged my arm. "Do not twist my words."

"Did she want to become a monster? Was turning all red-eyed and bitey her ultimate plan?"

He shook his head. "She must have wanted to control the Whisperer, perhaps all three of us. Something went wrong with her plan."

"You suspected she was involved."

"You were so unaware when I woke in your bed. All of my other guides summoned me, expected me. At first you were groggy and then you merely thought I was an easy lay."

I had to grin when he repeated the easy lay thing. I seemed to remember mumbling that when I'd first woken up. "I thought you'd come home with me from a party and I'd…somehow passed out and forgotten or you were a set up over my birthday."

"You couldn't let yourself see I was real."

That was just too close to home.

"What could she gain if she somehow had control over the Whisperer?" I asked.

Frey rubbed his right eyebrow, lips pursed. "She could use its energy to influence others, to gain power or wealth. It is not the first time someone has tried." He gave me a sober look. "There is no saving her, Bailey, not if she invited it."

I nodded. "I figured." I chewed my lip. "I, uh, told her I was going to meet you guys at Bono's for coffee.

That creature intercepting me wasn't an accident. She sent it."

"This knowledge hurts you."

I pulled out the flash drive I'd inserted in Professor Dunbar's computer, stuffed it and some papers into a plastic bag from the kitchen. "It was her Darth Vader moment. She failed."

"Darth Vader?"

"I'll fill you in later. Look, it's too dark and spooky to try to get out on that rock right now and retrieve the drawing if she stashed it there, so I vote we head back to my place."

Frey was on his feet. "It would be good to lie there with you."

"Just remember, no furs."

"You will keep me warm, yes?" I knew he was teasing me to try to help lighten things.

"I'd be happy to keep you warm. I'm thinking we'll hit the big sunken tub upstairs. You'll totally love it."

I shut down the desktop and Frey dressed and I picked up my still-wet shoes and socks. We made a dash for the car and Frey didn't make a big deal of folding back inside it into a cute Viking sandwich. I think he was too relieved we hadn't been attacked as we made a break for it.

But I felt something watching us through the swirling fog. And I knew it wasn't over.

Frey ran a hand over a cedar pillar as I unlocked the door to my house. "Hey, if you got stranded here, maybe you could build stuff," I said. "Log cabins, boats."

He gave me a startled look. "I like to build."

"Yeah, I had that sense. You remind me a bit of my Dad. He had an appreciation for natural materials, wood, stone. You really lit up when you saw my house. Even the carpet is woven sisal."

Frey nodded.

"I've missed that about him." I switched on more lights, not liking the look of the fog that was creeping up from the rocky beach below. "It would be nice seeing you using a hammer instead of that sword."

"You would wish me to be other than what I am," Frey said. "A guardian."

Bull's eye. "Well, it's kind of a depressing gig."

"It is you who is depressed."

I headed to the top floor and Frey followed me. He kept glancing out the windows at the fog. It seemed almost to scratch against the glass. "You have many totems here. It will serve as protection."

"Totems?" We were in the bathroom, which was about the size of my dorm room. Damn, I missed the place. Usually I was a shower man, but when I had a cold or felt like shit, there was nothing like hot jets.

"The…" Frey gestured to a framed watercolour of the bay I'd done when I was twelve. "The things made by you and others. They emanate strong protective energy."

"Whoa, that's a really interesting take on art and craft, that it originated like fire, to protect people, to make a circle," I mused. I loved that idea. I'd have to do a paper on it for Professor Dunbar. She'd be—

But she wouldn't be impressed. She was now a monster with a single consonant vocabulary.

I turned on the hot water and watched it flow out of the fancy waterfall copper tap. "You have to take your clothes off—" But when I turned to look at Frey, he'd already done it. "You know, the stripper thing is an excellent qualification in a boyfriend."

He raised his brows and then looked down at his body. "You like to look at my muscles."

I laughed. "Oh, yeah. And a lot of other things. Feel free not to wear clothing when we're alone together."

He looked smug but then wary as I led him to the bathtub. "It is a large pond."

"Can't swim?"

"I can. Why would I do so?"

"Hey, you were pretty clean when we first, you know, met. So you must bathe."

"Of course I bathe." He looked offended. "I do not overcome other warriors in battle with my smell."

"You smelt of campfire and earth." I tried to loop my arms around him, drag him closer to the tub, but he was as undraggable as a tree stump. I tried another method, nibbling on his earlobe. He sucked in a breath and his big hands tightened on my body.

"Bailey." He pushed me back so he could yank at my T-shirt. "When I am unclothed, I want…"

"Yes?" I kissed his neck.

"I want you unclothed also." It wasn't long before I was naked. I stepped into the water, settled near the jets and let out a long, luxurious sound. Frey's eyes widened and then he looked put out, probably because the sound I made was like one he could draw from me. He was jealous of the hot swirling water.

I grinned at him and he plunked in, hissing in a breath. "This!"

"Yeah, it's pretty cool."

He shook his head. "No, Bailey, it is hot."

His eyelashes fell and I knew I was in for it. My heartbeat thundered as he climbed over me, took my erection in his grasp.

I wrapped one leg around his hip while I kissed him. He took both our hard-ons, rubbing them together, killing me slowly.

"You are so hot," I muttered against his damp skin. "The way you tower over me, the sword, the calluses on your hands, the way your hair falls around your face. And Jesus, your eyes."

They looked at me now, into me, as he kissed me back, rutting with me. God, was there anything more perfect then my prick in his hand, rubbing velvety against his cock?

"I know we have this thing going on, creatures, darkness, but when you look at me like that, I just want you to fuck me." I shook my head. "No, that's not entirely honest. I want you to fuck me all the time."

"You are very eager to be a woman for me."

I frowned, still thrown by his archaic phrasing. "Um, yeah."

"I have never had a boy of my very own."

"No?"

"If I had met you in my time, I would have taken you."

"I would have been English, maybe a Celt," I said, spinning out the fantasy. Hell, I'd read tons of historical romances featuring hot, conquering Vikings. "You take me as your captive. Um…there'd have to be conflict. Oh, I know, your father was betrayed by my father. Well, he wasn't really, but you don't know that and they're both dead. So you capture me to 'punish' me by making me your kitchen slave. It's usually something humiliating so we fight a lot."

He stared at me, obviously enraptured as much by my storytelling ability as my hot little body. I grinned, loving being with him. The soothing water, the vivid blue eyes, his complete earnestness.

"We fight a lot?" he prompted when I lost myself in the feel of him gently thrusting against me, his hand gloving us both so perfectly.

"Yeah, I drive you crazy. I'm defiant and I keep trying to escape and…you want me. You're crazy for me, but I'm a virgin and you don't want to frighten me with your unnatural passions."

"I would not care if you were a virgin if you looked at me the way you do, Bailey," Frey grumbled. "I would tumble you hard."

"Ohhhhh." I bit my lip and arched into him, both the thought of being tumbled hard by my Viking and the feel of what he was doing pushing me to the edge. "Frey!"

"I will attend you," he whispered.

And did he. He moved his hips, rocking with the water, heating me almost lazily but with the intensity of a blowtorch. He was not playful. His hands caged my face and he stared into my eyes, trapping me.

"Don't!" I choked.

He did not relent. He did not let me go.

"I don't do it this way. I don't look in someone's eyes when I—"

"Come for me," he growled. "Burn for me."

I couldn't hold back. I thrust against him, the water churning over the lip of the tub, my eyes wide and naked as I came for him, as he found another way to conquer me.

Chapter Nine

This time I had no choice but to let him hold me since I'd basically collapsed against the side of the tub. He was all that was keeping my head above water, though I wasn't too sure about that in the metaphorical sense.

I was going under.

"Nice Viking," I mumbled. "Sexy Viking."

"I will tend you now."

"Oh yeah. Except any more tending and you might kill me." But I'd die with an X-rated smile on my face.

He manoeuvred me around and picked up some soap, sniffed it and then used it on my back. I let out a long sigh as water continued to pour from the recycling tub Mom had installed after I moved out. It was pretty cool, spilling over the copper edges and down the drain.

"This is not a very earth-friendly pool," he said and I laughed at the unexpectedness of his comment. I looked over my shoulder at him. He was smiling at me so I knew he was teasing.

"You heard that one from Candy."

"She said you were earth-friendly." His brow furrowed. "I'm still not sure I completely understand that. Why do you have to be friendly with dirt?"

"Well, um, not to be all literal and boring, but the water in the tub gets recycled into our garden hose so we can use it in the green house and gardens," I said. "And I'd get real friendly with dirt if you and I ever entered a mud wrestling contest." I grinned as that fantasy popped into my head. I'd lose of course, but Frey all slick and muddy and naked…

"Bailey." He smacked my hip. I guess he'd noticed I was perking up.

"Hey, young college man here," I said. "And what's your excuse?" I could feel his freshly interested cock poking against one ass cheek.

His eyes were half closed as he thrust against me. "I am a virile warrior."

"You're adorable."

He didn't look as if he cared for that description. He frowned at me thunderously and I laughed. "Sorry, it's just you're a bit geeky sometimes. I bet you'd be a hit with a medieval fantasy group."

"You have too much energy," Frey said in a silky voice, so I knew I was in trouble.

He hefted me from the water and threw me over his shoulder.

"Uh!" I gripped him, both of us dripping. "Frey, for fuck's sake…" Another swat on my abused backside. "Hey, ease up, that hurt!"

"I will tame you in your furs," Frey said and suddenly I was all for being tamed.

"First door on the left." My bedroom looked funny upside down since my Mom had taken to using it as an extra storage room for her crafts. I glimpsed the stacked tins of natural dyes on my old desk and some of the ochres she mixed with fresh soy bean milk, the colours vivid as eye shadow, blues, violets, fern greens.

And on my bed lay curls of washed wool, sorted and waiting to be spun.

Frey smirked at me. "You have furs."

"I'll never live it down." I hit the bed and shoved the clouds of wool off my bedspread with my heels and then Frey was on me, kissing me ardently. I'd never had a lover who was so intent on me. Usually one trip to a bathroom stall or a closet was enough and I'd got too jaded to follow a guy around afterwards, all dopey.

I knew the score.

But maybe Frey didn't because when my legs wound around his like hungry ivy he just grunted approval, kissing and nipping my neck while my head fell back. He tugged my hair, forcing me to look into his eyes again, but this time, though my throat tightened, I didn't try to fight.

"There's something in the drawer we need."

He opened it cautiously, as if something monstrous might spring free. After the day we'd had, I couldn't blame him. I took out the lube, closed my eyes and consciously worked to loosen my body as I readied myself to take him.

Frey helped me, his hand sweeping down, taking hold of my stiff penis, working me up and down so my body bowed off the bed. "*Fuck*!"

His lips burnt my skin, his white teeth nipped, his firm hands held me as he moved down my body and he swallowed my cock, sucking strongly while I bucked.

Then his mouth was on my opening, his tongue pushing inside.

I yelped and even he couldn't hold me down.

I fell off my bed and lay on the drifts of wool, staring up at him through my hair.

"You desired that," he said. "I felt the heat of your body, I heard your gasps. I did not misjudge, Bailey."

I swallowed, looked away. My body was still throbbing like a wild drum beat. Fuck yeah, I'd wanted that. "It freaked me out, okay?"

"Freaked you out?" he repeated and now the storm clouds were in his eyes, turning them to slate grey. He put his hands on his hips, assuming a warrior stance. "You will explain yourself."

A reluctant smile sprang to my lips. I could hear the word he hadn't tagged on, *You will explain yourself, boy.* He was trying to be civilised.

"It felt too good."

His brows rose.

I ducked my head. "No one ever bothered to do that for me before," I muttered, hitting closer to the truth this time.

"Bothered?" Frey looked perplexed. "To pleasure you?"

"I got off fine," I said. "Don't go feeling sorry for me."

"I do not." He laughed. "Now you are angry. That is good. I do not want a boy for my own who does not value himself."

"I'm not your boy. Reality check, Conan, this is temporary."

His eyes narrowed. "Do not call me by another's name. I do not like it. When you look at me, when you love me, you should only see me, feel *me*."

I was surprised the big lug didn't thump his chest.

"Christ, can't you see that's the problem?"

"Look at me, Bailey!" he thundered.

"All right, all right, don't yell! You'll bring the roof down."

"I do not care. If your house is splinters around us, I see only you." He dragged me close. "And you will see me."

I was seared by his hot blue gaze. Naked again.

I curled my arms around him, hid my face against his neck.

This he allowed and I squeezed my eyes shut until they didn't sting. Jesus, he really was turning me into a girl, though that was pretty sexist since my girl friends were all ass-kickers.

Listening to the steady thump-thump of his heartbeat soothed me. I couldn't resist licking him, savouring his salty flavour. His silken hair, damp on the ends, brushed my skin.

"Tell me why you pulled away from me. Do it now, Bailey."

"You're incredibly bossy, you know that?"

"I know what is good for my boy."

"Oh really? Let's add on arrogant."

"Bailey." He shook me. "I will know you."

"Damn it… You're leaving. All right? Enough said." I shoved my hair out of my eyes. "I want you safe and I want you with me." *Always.* Shit. I sucked in a deep breath. I couldn't think that way.

His swordsman's roughened palm cupped my cheek. Then he nuzzled me, his cheek to mine. Geez, it was dopey, but I liked it.

His gesture told me he didn't want to leave me either.

He cleared his throat. It sounded vaguely like the blast of a fog horn. "You liked my mouth upon you?"

Colour burnt my cheeks. Oh, hell, now I was blushing?

"I liked it. Too much," I said.

He studied me. "I would have your honesty and your honour."

He wanted me to bare my feelings. He could have made me do that by taking me in his mouth again, but he wanted me to talk to him.

"It was the hottest thing I've ever felt," I confessed.

He lifted me back onto my bed easily. Holding my gaze, he spread my thighs. My balls hung heavy, my cock hard and needy. I felt his breath on my opening. He drew out the moment, stroking my legs, kissing the mole above my knee.

"Please," I whimpered. "Frey, I need it."

"Tell me," he commanded. "I want to hear you."

He stabbed into me with his tongue, hot, wet, ravenous.

"Oh, fuck!" If he'd wanted to hear me, he'd got his wish. I think they could hear me in Tibet. "Frey!"

Frey wouldn't be rushed. He held me down when my hips lifted, forced me to take it as he lavished his attention on me, totally focused on tasting, sucking, making me loose and slutty.

I could feel him trembling.

"I can't!" My cock felt the lash every time he entered me with his tongue. I was going to shatter. I was closer to something that scared the shit out of me.

Him.

"Beautiful boy," he whispered, face strained. "Give."

I came, rolled under by this huge wave of love, coming just for him. I screamed as he penetrated me at last, gentle, so he rocked against me. He gave a war cry, taking me, his neck corded.

"I don't want to leave your body." He leant his forehead against mine. "If I had claimed you in my time, I would have chained you, kept you."

His words weren't exactly a Hallmark card, but I felt his heart thudding against mine, his hand gripping mine.

"What am I going to do now I've met the perfect historical romance hero?"

He grinned, a slash of satisfaction on his sweaty face. "I have ruined you for all other men. Candy said I would do such."

"Candy had a lot to say," I grumbled. "I'll be sure to get even with her."

The phone by my bed rang. I caught the portable. "Yo!"

"Moore, Jesus, what the fuck did you do to our door? It looks like you used a battering ram on it. Did you run out of coffee this morning?" my roommate, Jared Drake, groused.

"Shit!" I stiffened. "You didn't try to go into our residence, did you, Jair?"

"Nope, me and Miles are standing outside it right now. Uh, with Candy."

Candy. I wasn't surprised she'd shown up just when Jared had. She had an extra stalking sense when it came to Jared.

"Did the john back up? It stinks."

"No. Look, you better come out to my place. Don't try to go in there."

"No worries." I heard the disgust in Jared's voice. "Even after days of camping, I have no desire to go in there and try to shower."

"You can shower here. Bring Candy and Miles. I'll make us all dinner."

"You with this dude Candy's bent our ear about, the, uh, Norse guy?"

I smiled at the discomfort in Jared's voice. "He's here."

"Okay, we're coming, but no kissing and crap in front of us. Home rules apply."

"Home rules," I agreed. We had a rule that if we wanted to bring someone home to our dorm and make out, it was fine, but no one could do it in the shared space. I had no desire to see Jared or Miles with any of the campus honeys they brought home and they felt the same way about my men, not that there had been many.

After I cut the call I looked at Frey. His arms were folded and he was waiting on me. It reminded me that he really took this guide-business seriously. He trusted my judgement.

"That was one of my roommates, Jared," I told him. "You've been wearing some of his clothes. I told him not to go into the dorm room."

"That was wise." Frey nodded.

"I was also thinking…" I bit my lip and he leaned close and did it for me. "Mmmm." I blinked. "I was thinking that Jair and Miles and Candy could be reinforcements."

Frey cocked his head. "There has always been the guardian and the guide."

I raised a hand. "Listen, hear me out. First of all, from what you've said, sometimes the guide and the guardian don't exactly survive."

"No."

"Second, my friends…we've been through a lot together. You know, first year college when you feel like you'll never belong? Or, maybe you don't—"

"I know what it is to have no place, no friends," Frey said.

"Of course you do. You lost your village. I trust my friends, Frey. And with all this stuff happening, it just makes sense to ask for help. Jared and Miles are anthropology majors. That means they study different cultures, mythology. It might be useful." I couldn't resist reaching out and loosening one of his braids, which was messy. I smoothed his slick hair, re-braided it. He raised his chin, absorbing my attention as if I were his servant boy.

"Candy is a history and English double major. Last semester she read *Beowulf*."

"Stories tell us how to conduct ourselves, how to face death."

"Um, yeah, but maybe we can find a way to avoid the whole death thing. That's my point."

"If your friends come, you must dress yourself." Frey gave me a scandalised look, as if I was so sexy I'd drive them mad with lust if they got a look at my bare ass.

I laughed. "I plan on it." I went to my chest of drawers, rifled through until I found boxers. When Frey just lounged on the bed, I sent him a pair that had been a gift, and too big on me. He looked at the dancing elves and the chubby, laughing Santa on the boxers with clear suspicion.

"I would look better thus!" He gestured to his naked body. "You make sport of me, making me wear such uncomely clothing."

"Come on, the tie-dye had the side benefit of making you visible in the dark. And you're going to wear those because I say so," I told him. "I'm the guide, remember?"

Chapter Ten

"How long will it take your friends to muster their steeds and come to us here?" Frey asked with a gleam in his eye that gave me a restless, prickly feeling in my lower back.

"Muster their steeds?" I laughed and realised that I'd laughed more with Frey than any guy I'd ever dated. My men were for sex, for scratching that itch, but it was my friends I laughed with.

Until Frey.

He looked annoyed, as if he knew I found his phrasing quaint. Frey had a lot of pride.

"You know what it is I ask, Bailey." He shook me. "You know why."

"Again?" But I didn't mind. Geez, he really did have the stamina of a warrior and he couldn't seem to get enough of touching me, having me.

"You will be my *seiðmaðr*?" he whispered, kissing the side of my face. I closed my eyes, shivering at the thready, deliberate tease of his touch. I'd just come, but now I was heating up again. Why couldn't I get enough of him?

"What does that name mean, anyway?" I wasn't sure I wanted to know, given his outdated ideas, but I was too curious not to ask.

"A man who is a woman to other warriors."

"Okay, we need to talk about your outdated perspective—"

"Would you not like the role of my slave?"

"Depends. If it meant washing out your socks in a stream or something, I'll pass."

He lifted me onto his lap and then peeled down my boxers at the back, exposing my rear end. He ran his hand over my ass, caressing me. I hardened, needy again.

"It would mean that if I wanted to take you as a man does, you would make yourself available to me."

Okay, that was a sexy idea.

"So I'd be walking through your war camp, or whatever, and you'd grab me and—"

"I would do this." He swatted my ass.

"You have a gift..." I moaned as his hand found and stroked me. "For role-playing."

His lips curved. "I do not play at mastering you."

He spanked me.

He didn't ask me if it was a kink of mine, or negotiate rules or ask me for a safe word. He just...did it.

"Hey, ouch, this is—" It was a real spanking, intense, dominant. His hand warmed my ass without compromise, as if I were his slave, his boy. I squirmed, trying to soften it, trying to get off his lap. He struck me hard enough that tears stung my eyes. "Hey, this is me saying, *no*, asshole!" I hollered.

He stopped, but I knew it wasn't because of my protests. He shifted me so my sore bottom rubbed against his thighs. He was hard. Spanking me had excited him so that the length of his erection was outlined in a wet bloom against his boxers. His face was flushed.

"You don't spank someone when he says no!" I shoved him.

He pulled me in for a kiss. "Stop!" I punched his shoulder. I bit him.

I wrapped my legs around his waist.

He laughed and took my hard dick in his hand, caressing it possessively.

"That's not how we do things today! You have to talk to me, there are rules—"

"I will spank you when I wish it," he said. "I will do it in front of others if it is my pleasure to do so."

I could only stare at him, my heart thudding and my cock so hard I thought I'd die. My socialisation said this was all wrong but my primal self… I *loved* him. Oh shit. I'd gone and fallen for him. And my body had been made to be dominated by his.

He knew it. He wasn't going to back off.

"Bailey?" He wasn't asking me if I was okay with this. He was asking if I understood his rules.

"It's hard for me." I couldn't meet his eyes.

"I will own you. I will not have you hold yourself back from me," he said.

My arms were around him, tight, so tight. "I love the way you are with me," I whispered. "I've never been so turned on in my life." My face burnt, but I couldn't hold back. I wanted to lie in the dirt with his foot on my neck. Oh, Jesus!

He didn't do something an experienced Dom would do, like order me to kneel—because this wasn't role playing for him. I was his *seiðmaðr*. As long as he was with me, he'd do what he pleased with me.

"The spanking hurt." I couldn't help the spike of resentment.

"It was meant to." He'd meant to shock me from my complacency, from thinking I could shield myself from him. Casually, he pushed me to the floor, onto my hands and knees.

I looked over my shoulder at him, watched as he tugged down his boxers and then mounted me. One hand went to the back of my neck, pushing my head to the floor while my bottom stayed up.

He thrust inside me and I heard him grunt in pleasure.

He was making use of his boy, making his point that now I was his, he would take me for his own pleasure when he wanted.

I was wild to be taken, my cock aching, sensitised.

He was big and not easy for me to accommodate, but I did, the rough thrusts inflaming me so I scratched the hardwood.

He made no effort to touch me, to cater to me. This was all for him.

I loved that. I loved everything about being spanked and then fucked hard.

He gave another deep grunt of satisfaction and a rush of hot spend filled me. It was enough, along with his seeming indifference to whether I climaxed.

I came, squeezing his length, contractions of pleasure so long, painful…needed.

After, he picked me up, cradled me tenderly. My ass was sore, but that rawness was a reminder. He wanted me to feel his possession, to feel the transition we'd made from friends to lovers on his terms.

He was kind now.

"I'd rather you never did that in front of my friends," I said.

He studied me and then nodded. "It would hurt you. I do not wish to hurt you, beloved boy."

"No, that's not what you want. You want to keep me safe." My throat burnt. "You'd die for me."

"Of course," he said, stroking my hair.

"I…love you," I whispered.

He nodded again, as if his boy should love him.

I laughed shakily. "It's crazy. We just met. I shouldn't let myself feel this way. When you have to leave, if you get hurt, it will destroy me."

"Why shouldn't love destroy?" he asked calmly.

The ball in my chest ached. "You'll let it destroy you?"

"Yes," he said.

He wasn't telling me 'Bailey, I love you desperately, let's build a tree house together', but he was telling me he loved me.

I'd been empty and longing for someone. All my life. I'd wanted love to make me feel safe, to make me feel like a wonderful lover.

He'd given me love and it was ripping me apart.

"Lord Byron." I gave Jared my best formal bow when he entered my kitchen. His dark, brooding gaze lightened and he shoved some of that equally dark hair out of his eyes. He gave me the finger.

Candy and Miles came next, Miles' unshaven jaw and bed hair a match for Jared's.

"We shower and then we eat," Jared announced. "And then we talk about why we came home to an apartment that smells like a sewer."

I looked at Frey, who was calmly chopping up the herbs I'd found growing on the windowsill in the kitchen. They'd needed a little TLC, soaking in a basin to suck up some moisture, but they were probably safer to harvest than risking going back to the spooky greenhouse.

"Do you sense anything?" Frey asked me.

"Nothing more than I'm tired and hungry," I said.

He looked outdoors at the fog that continued to writhe through the woods like something from a Hollywood smoke machine. At the moment the big evil we were facing seemed content to just play with the scenery.

"Take your shower, boys," I said.

But when I looked over my shoulder, Jared and Miles were already gone. Candy was chewing her lip, looking after them.

"Jared didn't pump you?" I asked her.

She went beet red. "Excuse me?"

"I mean for *information.* Geez, everything with you is sex, sex, sex."

"I'm a healthy young woman. And no, both he and Miles are pretty flaked out from their camping deal. I think they're pissed because they think it's a plumbing thing and you don't want to own up to it."

I put some dim sum dumplings onto the frying pan, listened to them sizzle before I stuck broccoli and sliced carrots to roast in the oven.

"Jeez, I'm starving," Candy said, sitting down in one of the kitchen chairs. "I always forget your mom taught you to cook."

"Hello, this is my own recipe," I said.

"What student doesn't love dim sum?" she asked, reminding me of all the groggy Sunday mornings we'd gone out for some.

"Exactly."

"Anymore close encounters?" she asked me, watching Frey as he hefted the knife he'd been using on the herbs, twirling it mid-air and then catching it easily. He was such a show off. But he looked…well, damn good. Apparently having sex and being bossy agreed with him. I looked away from the flex of his muscles before I burnt the dumplings.

"Bailey, take five." Candy dragged me into the alcove next to the spiral staircase. Frey frowned and looked after us, but seemed to relax when we didn't go far.

"What?" I widened my eyes at her and then blew out a breath in exasperation. "You are so not going to ask me how things are going between me and Frey? News flash—there's more important stuff going down right now."

She pinched me.

"Because if you are, that is such a cliché. You might as well invite me to refresh my makeup with you in the john so we can talk about boys."

She said dryly, "If we go in your bathroom now, we'll not only talk about boys, we'll see them. And the only time you wear makeup is Hallowe'en."

"Exactly. Not that I don't look wonderful in eyeliner." I batted my eyelids.

"I'm sorry. You just seemed…well, devastated when we got here."

I swallowed thickly and took her in my arms.

"Now I'm really worried!" She socked my biceps.

"I had a Rosemary Rogers moment with Frey," I said.

Candy gaped at me. "He acted like a seventies romance hero, all taking you until you liked it?" She knew me so well, knew that had always been my secret fantasy.

I nodded.

"Oh no. You'll have no choice now but to fall for him."

"I have," I admitted, miserable.

"Oh honey." She hugged me and I absorbed her closeness, her familiar comfort.

"It hurts, Candy. I can see why we stuck to reading about love because the real thing *sucks*."

"But is the sex as good as in the books?"

"Better," I croaked.

"Well, at least you've got that. Bailey…" She tugged my hair and I looked at her. "This is no time to wimp out! Time to be a romance hero. Time to write your happy ending."

"It's easy in books. You know that's guaranteed or you can bitch about it on Goodreads," I moaned. "It's depressing as hell livin' it."

"Man up." Candy poked me. "You're crazy about Frey. What are you going to do to keep your man with you?"

Jared joined us, hair damp and silky. His amber-brown eyes flicked to Candy and then to me. He smiled. "Having fun, girlfriends?"

"Fuck you." But I felt better, as he'd meant me to.

Miles looked sleepy, like he needed to roll back into bed. He always looked that way, hiding a razor mind. I felt better, knowing I had him on my side. Miles was patient and relentless. He'd once waited two years to get back at a jock who'd hounded him in high school. I shuddered as I remembered the guy screaming as he ran through the middle of campus naked and wearing a donkey mask.

"I better tell you what's up," I said. "Come on, this will go down easier with some red wine."

"Better be some of your Mom's," Jared said. "Yours is only good to mix with a salad."

Jared opened a really good Spanish wine and I filled my friends in on the attack in the greenhouse and what had gone down with Professor Dunbar at her townhouse.

"I knew that fog wasn't right," Jared said.

"Oh, please," Candy muttered.

"What?" Jared glared at her.

I think the stress of our situation was wearing on Candy. She wasn't using that irritating breathy voice she usually reserved for moments with Jared. And she glared right back at him.

"You're just suggestible. Bailey tells you something's out there and you've convinced yourself you sensed it beforehand. It's always foggy here. It's the Pacific Northwest."

"I don't think that is being suggestible." Jared pointed to the swirls of moisture wreathing the house. They looked as thick as the curls of wool in my bedroom. Definitely high creep factor.

She swallowed. "Okay, even for our climate that's…"

"So your drawing, Dunbar snagged that right off?" Miles interrupted.

I looked at him, seeing calculation behind the dull brown eyes.

"Yeah, she did."

"And you think she might have stored it in her garden pavillion?"

"Yep. Frey didn't feel it in the house. Apparently he can sense it, since it's the doorway." I looked at Frey. He was leaning against the counter, sipping wine from a coffee mug. Probably he found that more manly than one of Mom's slender, hand-blown glasses.

"Seems to me we should take your graphic away from her," Miles said. "We take it back, make it work for us."

Frey straightened. "Never have I attempted such. The guide and the guardian are always hunted."

"We've been attacked three times," I said. "It's only a matter of time before they pick one of us off."

Why can't love destroy? Frey had asked me. This wasn't a game. This was all or nothing.

I didn't have any answers. If I had powers as a guide, they weren't kicking in. I didn't know what to do next, so I went with instinct.

Heart thudding, I said, "Let's take the fight to them."

Chapter Eleven

We started with dim sum and Molotov cocktails.

"Came in handy, finishing two bottles of wine," Miles said as he stuffed a rag in the bottle he'd prepared. Frey was helping him, fascinated by the procedure.

"I knew of Greek fire, of catapults like the Romans used," he said.

"We're not staging the siege of Troy," I said dryly.

Frey looked disappointed. "No. We do not make siege."

"Hey, that's a good thing. War is bad," Candy said.

"We must be friendly with dirt and not fight. Your world is strange."

"How did a vegetarian tree-hugger wind up with Conan?" Candy asked me.

"Fate," I said.

"I am not Conan!" Frey bellowed. He pointed his sword at me. "I will challenge this former lover of yours to a duel at the first opportunity, guide, and put him down. He will not touch you."

"As adorable as your bloodthirsty attitude is, I have to tell you there is no Conan in my past."

Frey glowered at me. "There will be none in your future."

"I think it's pretty unlikely." I didn't think I was breaking the house rules by grazing a finger over the back of Frey's hand. "You're my only barbarian lover."

He grunted, but I liked his jealousy. I wasn't disposable to him. I was his boy. *His.*

"Is this romantic interlude over, or do you need more time with your boyfriend?" Miles asked.

"Nope, I think that part of our evening has run its course," I said.

"Okay then, back to danger and death."

"We need to strike," Frey said, obviously in tune with Miles. "Bailey and I will find his drawing. You and Jared will come with us. Candy…" He looked at her. "Will stay here."

"What?" She gave me an indignant look. "Oh, I'll just prepare bandages for the wounded."

Frey nodded. "Yes."

"Bailey!" she squeaked.

But I really didn't want her to come. I rubbed the back of my neck and pulled Frey into the alcove.

"Don't think I don't know you two are plotting!" Candy growled.

"One thing that has changed with the times is women are equals," I said. "They go into combat situations, they hold jobs."

Frey raised an eyebrow. "So we'll just have to be sneaky in the way we keep her safe."

"Yes," I said.

"I am not staying behind!" Candy continued hotly. "Why should you two have all the fun?"

"Fun? Yeah, it's been a laugh a minute being attacked at unexpected intervals by weird creatures from another dimension," I said.

"I think Candy should stay here," Miles intervened in a mild voice.

"Why is that?" Candy demanded suspiciously. It was just her tough luck that she was outnumbered by four men who were not going to see her hurt.

"Because some of the manifestations so far have been localised in this house," Miles said. "Professor Dunbar may show up here while we're attempting to find Bailey's graphic. Someone needs to keep watch."

"That doesn't sound very exciting."

Miles pointed to the heavy fog rolling beyond the window pane.

"Well…" She swallowed. "There is that. Do you think it'll let up once you guys go?"

Miles eyes didn't light with triumph. He was one smooth dude. "No way to know. You'll have to watch, take notes. It could come in handy later, mapping this thing out."

She nodded. "All right, but I grew up watching Buffy. It's a let down to just…stay here."

"Buffy's sidekicks ended up being very powerful," Miles said. "But it takes practice."

"You watch Buffy?" She gave him a surprised look, as if she'd never paid much attention to him before. Candy was a Buffy fanatic.

"Buffy's hot, though I preferred Willow, myself."

"Mmmmm."

"Is there anything we can do to make this place more secure while we're gone?" Miles asked.

"A circle of salt," Frey said. "Sea salt is best."

"We have lots of that thanks to my Mom's silk painting." It was an ingredient she used not only to mix her dye recipes, but to add texture to the works themselves, so we had enough salt to sink a battleship. "But it'll take time to circle the house and the damp weather will dissolve it quickly," I said.

"No need to use it like that," Miles said. "Just set up shop somewhere like the kitchen and outline the inner room." He gave Candy a hard look. "And you have to stay in the circle."

Candy grimaced. "I know, I know. In movies and books, the dumb heroine always leaves the circle and something happens to her."

"Right," Miles said. "And you're not dumb."

"No." She gave him a speculative look. I realised that she hadn't asked Jared's opinion once. She seemed focused on Miles.

Huh. Maybe my girlfriend was wising up. Miles might not have Jared's looks, but he was a true Scorpio man, the secretly sexy sort. If he'd been into guys, I'd have tumbled him myself.

Miles and I used measuring cups and divided a sack of sea salt, spilling the contents patiently in a circle. Within the perimeter, Candy had TV, radio and a land-line phone. Still, it was hard to leave her behind. I could take just about anything, but not losing her.

"She'll be safe," Frey said, squeezing my arm as we walked cautiously to my car. Jared and Miles would take their own, a beater they shared that was just sturdy enough for their off-road trips.

"Did you by any chance have a sister? You know, way back when."

Frey's face was expressionless. "I did, yes."

"I'm sorry."

"It was a long time ago."

No, I thought, it was yesterday. It was why he was the guardian. He'd lost his family, his centre.

"The fog isn't letting up. We'll have to crawl on the road," I said.

Frey cranked his body in half and sat beside me, watching with interest as I started the car. I knew if he stayed here a while, he'd hit me up for driving lessons, and wouldn't that be something, teaching a Viking warrior how to drive?

I shuddered, imagining him bellowing at me as he fought to keep to the speed limit.

"I can't see the house," Frey said.

Jesus. We'd just pulled out and all the landmarks had been swallowed by swirling mist.

"I need to open the windows to check where I'm going." Ahead of the car was a bit of asphalt and the blank canvas of the fog. Behind us I thought I could make out the headlights from Jared and Miles' car.

I slammed the breaks.

The car skidded and I pumped the breaks, fighting momentum.

Frey smacked the windshield.

We lurched to a stop.

"Fuck!" I grabbed Frey's head, checking out the break in the skin on his forehead. He was going to have one hell of a bruise. "You didn't put on the seatbelt. Didn't I tell you—"

"It is just a knock."

"You wouldn't have one if you'd worn the belt like I told you!"

"Guide." His voice calm, still as a pool of rainwater.

"Yeah, okay." My hand was shaking as I pulled the key from the lock. "We're okay. We didn't go off the road."

We got out of the car, looked at the cedar lying across the road, branches like bristling spines. I could smell the tang of fresh wood.

"This has just toppled. What are the chances that's a coincidence?" I asked.

Frey said nothing.

"Yeah, didn't think so. Okay, Professor Dunbar's place isn't far as the crow flies. We can walk. But first we should wait for Jared and Miles…"

"We cannot." Frey had his sword in his hand. "You know we cannot."

Brush moved behind us, swaying in what could have been the damp sea breeze, but I knew it was more.

"Hang on." I picked up a fallen cedar branch, used it to scratch an arrow in the mud by the car. Then I broke off the front of the stick, making a sharpened point.

"We must move!"

We ran. Into the woods and over mossy rock with fingers of fog whirling an idle dance. The air tasted like dripping ice. My frantic breath gusted out in spurts as I jumped over a fallen tree. I could smell the sea, hear the distinctive wet sounds of the ocean lapping at the beach below.

And through the trees, through the mist, I heard the snap of twigs and soft, furtive footfalls. The flash of eyes, red as Christmas lights.

"More than one," I panted to Frey.

"Three," he said. "It has killed and bred. If it is allowed to stay here, there will be creatures unnumbered." He gripped my arm. "Go to the summer house. Find the drawing you made. You are the guide. You are the only one who can summon what has used the door, force it from this world."

"What about you?"

"I will stay."

Stay and fight what hunted us. Keep them from me.

"Can't leave you." His braid was messy again. His eyes were the colour of cold steel in the half light.

"Go and be well, guide," he said. "I will follow if I can."

A shadow leapt between us and he swung his sword. Teeth jagged as spikes, dripping with saliva. Fury in the bunched muscles, the feral eyes.

"Frey!"

"Go!"

I ran, I left him. I heard a scream behind me, high and pained. The creature or my lover?

I was in passing shape, but the mist pooled over the ground, making footing treacherous. I stumbled, nearly losing the sharpened stake. Behind me I glimpsed something silent and quick leaping with the eerie silence of flowing liquid over the deadfall.

I made it to the top of the steep rise looking over Professor Dunbar's town house. I hesitated, looking for a safe way down. Hot breath hit my neck. I felt it behind me.

I let go, dropped, falling, hitting rock, rolling, bouncing…

I slammed into the road in a heap. Grabbed my chest. Oh, shit.

I heard crashing sounds behind me. Saw the back of my hand greased red with blood as I used it to heft myself back on my feet.

I staggered, limping.

Behind me, the Shadow creature stood in the centre of the asphalt, glowing eyes fixed on me. The sharpened branch was gone. I had nothing.

It seemed to know, lips twisting in a toothy smile as it trotted towards me.

I hissed out a breath as I bent down, grabbed a rock.

A horn blasted.

Jared threw open the rusty door of his Dodge sedan. "Get in!"

I heard the racing click of claws behind me, dived into the passenger side, managed to yank the door closed. "Oh, God, oh *fuck!*"

The thing hit the car door, claws scrabbling.

Miles spun the car around, worn out tyres squealing in a high, scared sound. The thing clung to the car, staring at me.

"Hang on!" Miles warned coolly.

We drove into granite, the wall of the sloping mountain that met the road. A shriek and the smear of blood, broken glass.

"Are you hurt?" Miles demanded.

"Rib," I said. "Not sure if it's busted."

"If it's busted, you'd know," he said.

Jared was looking over his shoulder behind us. His face was pale when he turned around and faced me and Miles. "Nice job creaming that thing," he told Miles. He looked at me. "You look like shit."

The street lamps seemed to streak by like stars in hyperspace.

"Bailey!"

"Uh… C'est what?" I managed.

"He's speaking in French and English," Jared said. "Not a good sign."

The engine wasn't running. I sat up and wished I hadn't when nausea rolled through me. I breathed in shallowly so I didn't bring on the red pain in my ribs. I couldn't imagine how it would feel if I puked my guts out like my body wanted.

We were parked outside Professor Dunbar's town house. The door stood open. Inside a light moved from window to window gleefully, like a supernatural tennis ball.

"Okay, that's nice and creepy," Jared said. "Where's Thor?"

"He'd hate being called that," I said. "He's…" I shook my head. Had those things taken Frey down? Was he lying broken in the woods?

"Where's this summer house?" Miles asked, pulling out his knapsack. He steadied me as I got painfully out of the back of the car.

"On the rocks in front of her place," I said.

"Okay, you and Jared make for it."

"What about you?" I didn't want to leave another person I cared about behind.

Miles didn't spare me a glance as he headed for the light show in the townhouse. "How can I resist? I'll catch up."

Jared and I ran around the side of the house and I felt the fog like wet fingers touching my exposed skin. My side hurt, so I banded an arm around it in support.

"You'll need to get those ribs wrapped," Jared said, reminding me he'd played rugby for years.

"Yeah." The pavillion was dark, in contrast to the spooky main house. It sat on the rock in silhouette, surrounded by starshine and lapping water.

"Looks too easy," Jared said. "Maybe the drawing isn't here."

I shrugged then winced when the movement hurt my sore ribs. "No idea. Only one way to find out."

We walked carefully over the wooden bridge and climbed the steep rough surface of the granite, poking up like the bones of a long-dead dragon.

The summer house was one of those simple cedar designs made from a kit, round, with pillars and slats and benches, open to the sea breeze. Professor Dunbar had furnished it with wicker that had gone silvery, splotched with lichen. A dried-flower wreath hung from a spotted mirror, reflecting the sleeping sea.

"The benches," I said, then knelt painfully beside the first. Each one could be raised, with storage under the lid. I found some mouldy needlepoint and a tangle of wool. Jared tossed things from the one he'd taken as I crawled to the next. A heavy silver teapot of Indian design, blackened from lack of use and a couple of chipped Royal Doulton cups.

"Nothing." And no more benches.

I felt defeat rising in my chest. I was tired, Frey was missing, and I hurt.

I'd hung my hopes on finding something out here.

"Bailey, what if it's underneath the summer house?" Jared asked.

He shifted the rug and I saw the little trap door that had been underneath it. Likely there wasn't much under there but wolf spiders and mice, and boy, wasn't I looking forward to finding out.

Suddenly the house behind us lit up, illuminating the night like an X-Ray.

"I think it knows we're out here," Jared said.

Chapter Twelve

"Means we're on to something." We lifted the trap door together. It was heavy and rattled against the wood floor after we'd pried it free.

"Me," I said, before Jared could take point. "I started all this. The drawing is mine." And I wanted to head into that wet hole under the summer house about as much as I wanted to smash my fingers with a hammer, but I had to do this.

I pulled out a small flashlight, flicked it on. My ribs protested with an exquisite symphony of pain as I wiggled down, feeling the cool damp rock scraping my cheek. Not much room down here, but maybe enough for a small woman to stash something.

I felt a pulse, and my fingertips tingled. Something was here. Something mine. It was the same tie in the gut I'd felt lying under Frey, looking into his eyes for the first time.

But knowing and finding were two different things.

I was caged under the wooden floor, laced with silty cobwebs. Something soft and furry brushed my arm.

"Find it?" Jared yelled impatiently from above me.

"I just got down here," I grumbled.

"Well, the light show in the house went out. I'm thinking that's not a good sign," he said. "So hurry the fuck up."

I squirmed forward, every movement rubbing my sore ribs painfully together so breathing hurt. Moisture slicked the back of my neck. What if I got trapped down here?

I reached the side of the structure. Nothing. But at least the sea air blew through a shrub and into the space, making me feel less confined.

Above me I heard a heavy thud.

"Jared?" I called. My voice sounded husky to my own ears.

Jared didn't reply.

Urgency beat in my blood like a war drum. I had to find it. I crawled around the circumference, but still I couldn't see anything but rock and the stirring weeds.

A shadow blocked the light from the open trap door. "Bailey?" The voice that called wasn't Jared's. It was low and crooning, sweet like rotting pastry. "I know you're down there."

With nothing to lose, I shoved my hand into the bushes beside me. I didn't hope to find anything now, but maybe I could pull myself free. Ow! Holly leaves. Great, just great. I sucked on my filthy pricked finger and prepared to move on, find another spot for escape.

But wasn't holly a natural barrier? I remembered reading about mazes using it to guard the centre and the treasure.

I groped, got another prick from a fallen leaf and then touched something metal.

A chest.

It grated against the rock as I pulled it to me.

"Bailey…" the voice sang, cheerful as a cereal box ad. "Don't make me come after yoooou."

The box creaked open and there it was, my burnt graphic, tied in a scroll with black ribbon. I took it, shoving it down my T-shirt as I began to crawl for a gap. I was definitely not going to try to climb back through the trap door with that friendly voice calling for me.

I wiggled through the opening, gasping at the pain in my side. I staggered to my feet and looked for Jared. Right off I saw him. He was lying on his side, blood running from his hairline.

Professor Dunbar stood over him, smiling at me. "Let's you and I have a talk," she said, just as if I'd shown up at her office on campus.

"What did you do to him?"

"Oh, I didn't do that," she said. "It did." She pointed to one of the toothy Shadow creatures, which padded out of the tall grass and knelt like a pet at her feet.

"Let me guess, if I open the door, you have to leave this world because you…what? Sold yourself to the Whisperer?"

"Whisperer," Professor Dunbar scoffed, frosty blue eyes giving me a disapproving look. She certainly seemed more like herself and less like the dripping evil-eyed thing Frey and I had first encountered. And why wasn't that reassuring? "Very dramatic. The energy cloud has a name that has to be sung."

"I doubt I could sing right now."

"No, you couldn't. But if you got hurt, it's your own fault, isn't it?" she snapped. "What do you know about anything? You're a student. You're self-absorbed when you aren't obsessed with sex. You have it all in front of you. You aren't counting down to sixty without meeting your ambitions."

"My Mom's counting down to sixty but she hasn't swallowed the big evil."

"Your mother is content to spin and dye wool and spend time in her organic garden when she isn't travelling. She doesn't need to be remembered. Do you think it's easy to teach in a second-rate university when I could have written books, taught in the finest schools?"

"So why didn't you?"

"I…" She blinked. The thing at her feet never looked away from me, body quivering. "I had plenty of time. I thought—but I was like you, Bailey. I was consumed with the moment."

"Sounds like you were just like the students you despise."

"I woke up when I was passed over for something I deserved." She glared at me. "Even with everything that's happening, what are you most worried about?" She kicked Jared. "Your little friends. Your virile new boyfriend."

"He is pretty virile," I agreed. "He also has an honest heart."

"Good for him. The powers will find another guardian now he's fallen," she said. "Oh, you didn't know? My friends tore him to shreds in the woods."

I don't know what my face revealed, but she laughed.

"I don't believe you." I couldn't. The idea of Frey dead… I just couldn't.

"Whatever, as you students are fond of saying," she said. "Down to business. You have my graphic. I want it back."

I reached under my shirt and grabbed hold of it possessively. "No. You may have tricked me into making it. I may be the typical feckless student, but you can't have it."

Her eyes narrowed.

"You knew it was a formula, whatever you want to call it, to call those creatures to our world, but you didn't have the gumption to do it yourself. You manipulated me into doing it for you."

"You were easy to manipulate. You're ambitious, not that you'll probably go anywhere. You might end up travelling to India and helping people get rid of toxic dye waste like your mother."

"It's important work," I said. "Maybe it won't make her famous, but it helps people, the environment."

"Jesus, you're just like her." Professor Dunbar shook her head. "Since you're such an unexpected do-gooder for a student, I will admit I had some trouble subduing this…alternative personality I'm carrying. But now I'm fine. There's no need to open the door, send it back. You can let me finish what I've started. Let me do that and you and your friends won't get hurt."

I looked at the wolverine thing at her feet. "Frey said the Shadow creatures are breeding. To do that, they have to feed, right?"

She gave me a blank look.

"What, it never occurred to you? How long until we read about missing students on campus, or here in town?"

"You are not going to do this, you are not going to screw something up you don't understand. Life is not shades of black and white," she snarled.

The scroll in my hand felt warm in the wet chill. My fingertips prickled again. I had an urge to open it, to look at the undulating design.

"Wha—?" Jared lifted his head, shook it.

"Don't," I told Professor Dunbar. "If you hurt him—"

Something rattled on the floor in the corner of the summerhouse.

"Oh shit!" I lunged for Jared as the Molotov cocktail Miles had prepared before we left the house burst into flame, shooting up one pillar.

Jared was in my arms, panting. I swiped at the blood on his face. "Well, hell, Miles," he grumped. "Took you a while."

Miles stood in silhouette, another bottle held ready. "Just let them go, Professor."

"Isn't it sweet, students ganging up against the establishment," she said. "Although I'm surprised you're joining in with them, Miles. I always took you as more intelligent than the other algae."

"Algae? That's an insult, right?" Jared huffed. "Hey!"

"You can all go if you give me that graphic, Bailey." She held out her hand for it.

"No!"

I knew that voice. It was strung in my gut, it was locked in my voice.

Frey hobbled into the pool of light from the burning pillar. His face was scratched, one vivid blue eye swollen almost shut. His lean hand covered his stomach, where blood oozed.

"Frey!"

His gaze snapped to mine, burnt me. "I am…well, guide."

Oh yeah, he was looking really well. I growled under my breath.

"You…are well also?"

"Peachy."

He looked confused, but I didn't have time for his literal-minded approach. The graphic was glowing now and when I looked at it, it seemed to float above the paper in 3D.

"Trippy!" Jared whispered.

"Surround the guide," Frey ordered Miles and Jared. "Protect him with your very existence."

Miles was already there, having moved while our attention was on Frey. He was a sneaky bastard.

"Our very existence?" Jared repeated. "Dude…"

The drawing began to rotate like a carousel picking up speed.

"Bailey…" Frey's gaze held mine. "You know what to do."

Funnily enough I did. It was as weird as a complex answer to a fantastical math problem suddenly popping into my head. I could see the time wind, the probabilities, the actions and reactions playing out.

"I summon you!" I pointed to Professor Dunbar.

"No, I won't let you—" She was speeding up, colours streaming until she…just wasn't there anymore. A small stain of black smoke remained, burning my nose.

The Shadow creature leapt. Miles butted it back. "Hurry the fuck up!"

"I summon you!" My voice was stronger but Frey had the thing, jaws snapping as it twisted to try and bite him. I saw the creature blur, saw Frey's hand begin to dematerialise. "*No!*"

The matrix was mine. I could write it, I could make it what I wanted. The beast shot into hyperspace, but I held Frey. Sweat dripped down my face. I shook with the effort, feeling as if my gut would rip apart. But I held him.

"Guide..." His voice was heavy with the leaving. "Let me go."

"No. You...have a choice. You lost your centre, your family, but now you can have it again." I laid myself bare. I gave myself. "With me. With my friends."

"The vortex needs a guardian."

"So you'll just be a guardian while you live here. With me. My friends can even help out the next time you're summoned." I knew he had a choice, if he could let himself. "Listen, you can make a life here. I don't know what you'll do, if you'll build houses or... I don't care. I want you in my life. Nothing makes sense if I wake up with you one morning, fall for you, and you go away again."

He reached out for the wavering paper. I wasn't sure what his choice would be until he took my hand and it fluttered to the ground, discarded.

"You are my centre."

I grinned, because the way he said it reminded me so much of Arnie-speak. *YOU-R-my-CEN-tar*. But I was careful not to mention Arnie's name. Making Frey jealous might be fun sometimes, but not right now.

Anyway, I couldn't have talked because I was crushed in his arms and he was smeared with dried blood and I couldn't stop touching him, just touching him.

He kissed me.

And I was his centre.

"Hey, he gets the guy and I get battered and for what?" Jared groused.

"Shut up, dickhead," Miles said affectionately.

Epilogue

You'd think life would be one smooth happy-ever-after after meeting the man you were destined to love. Most of all, you'd think you could sleep in once in a friggin' while.

But nooo.

I woke, as I usually woke in my dorm room, under six-feet plus of sleepy golden muscle.

The Johanna Lindsey book we'd re-enacted the night before fell to the floor with a thump.

"Bailey, I will get you coffee."

I mumbled something, tried to swat him away.

"I will tend to you."

That had one eye opening. My body woke up quicker than I did and Frey had a handle on where, stroking me. "Mmmm."

"You have a class this morning."

"Why are there such things as morning classes?" I moaned, grabbing a pillow and covering my head with it.

"A warrior is eager to meet his day." Frey swatted my backside. "And I am eager, as always."

He kissed the knobs of my spine, licking, sucking, so that I forgot it was morning and I was so horny I was ready to hump the bed. "Frey!"

He turned me over and spread my legs and oh, boy, did he tend to me, taking me in his mouth, holding me down as I wiggled, laughing when I begged.

I came, but I didn't just climax as I had before meeting him. With Frey, I almost blacked out, so intense, colours flashing, warm, ruthless mouth, callused hands holding me, keeping me safe as he shot me high.

I was still panting, recovering from what really was the little death, when he pushed lube into me before mounting me.

I groaned as I accommodated him.

"You are well?" he asked, as he always did.

"If I tell you how well I am, you'll just get smug."

He grinned and began to move gently. Oh, yeah. It was going to be one of those mornings when he took his time. He lifted my arms above my head, held them there. He was all 'take charge' this morning, but when wasn't he?

Not that I was complaining…

"I'm taking the class with the new prof, the one who replaced Dunbar," I told him as he set me free long enough so I could score his back tenderly with my nails. He likes to wear my marks. He even shows them off, which is incredibly embarrassing but also makes me weirdly proud.

"You will do well in this class! I will put my energy into you," he bellowed. And then he stopped playing with me and he took me. Conquered me.

I quivered under him when he was done with me. And he looked smug, damn it.

"What about that coffee you mentioned?" I'd taught him how to make it. He drank it all the time, so it had been a necessity.

"I met another of your former lovers," Frey said, getting out of bed and opening the door. I watched him, stared at his ass as he made us coffee. Then his words penetrated. Oh shit!

"Frey…" I began carefully. "You didn't challenge this one to a duel, did you?" I'd have to hide his sword again. I still remembered the first time one of my asshole exes had made a crack about how easy I was to Frey.

"I let him live, my guide," he said. "Killing him and leaving his guts spread over campus would have been messy, yes?" He looked at me with bright blue eyes.

"Yeah." Damn, the big lug's jealousy was not adorable. I cleared my throat. If I got too mushy, Miles and Jared wouldn't let me hear the end of it. I knew Frey's bellowing during sex probably had them half awake. "You going into the shop this morning?"

"Yes, I am." His eyes were even brighter as he brought back perfectly made coffee and we shared from the same mug. "Candy is a wondrous friend to have found me this place of work."

Frey worked in a motorcycle showroom and repair shop. Who knew, but he was obsessed with motorcycles. He'd got his licence recently thanks to some underhand computer work on Miles' part. God knew what my stealthy friend had pulled, but Frey had ID now. One day Miles would be running the CIA or something. He was one scary dude.

"Miles and Candy want to see a movie with us tonight," I said.

"He is a good master for her," Frey said and I choked on my coffee.

"Ah, Frey... Didn't we have that little talk about women's liberation and stuff? Don't call him her master, not in her hearing anyway."

"Miles smiles when I call him such," Frey said.

I had to laugh. "It's your funeral."

Frey took my hand. "I will walk you to class, yes, my *seiðmaðr?"*

"Yeah," I said. "I guess that'd be all right."

THE ALIEN IN MY KITCHEN

Dedication

To my Wednesday morning class. Hatha yoga, cookies, meditation and green tea—and you all keep me laughing. Namaste.

Chapter One

I learn by going where I have to go
– Theodore Roethke

"What now?" I asked my best friend, Esmeralda Marks, EZ for short. She'd been calling me nonstop all afternoon. You'd think I'd never got the flu before. Okay, not just the flu, but some kind of modified flu-bomb that was genetically engineered to bring me down and make me beg.

"Mitchell Blake, don't you dare hang up!" she screeched.

"Ouch! Don't yell!" I thrust the BlackBerry away from my face. At her volume, I decided I was safer putting it on speaker and placing it on the kitchen counter of my swanky dirty-dish-buried kitchen.

"Mitch, I'm serious."

Something in her tone caught my muzzy attention. I dumped a load of plates into the soapy water. Since I was stuck missing classes today because I was still sick, I figured I should catch up on the chores my experiments usually eclipsed.

"You're serious..." I prompted, my gut twisting when I heard her audible swallow on the phone. "You aren't pregnant, are you?" She was my best friend, and despite her nickname, EZ, she wasn't. But her voice was all about bad news.

"No, I'm not pregnant. Why would you think that?" She sounded cross.

"I don't know. But if you were, we could raise the kid together. I could be the gay-best-friend daddy. It'd be cool. They'd make a movie—you know, showing us struggling with diapers and baby poop and going on dates with the wrong people but then, because it's Hollywood, I'd suddenly realise I was straight and we'd wind up together."

She laughed. "Mitch, you are such a weird guy."

"Hey, it's my pitch for the day."

"You haven't been watching the news?"

I blinked, washing out a serving bowl. I had no memory of using it to serve anything to company. I probably had it for instant noodles when I'd run out of clean plates. "Nope. News free. I was busy with this new experiment, calculating the velocity of mould growing on rocks when speeding through a vacuum."

"Uh-huh." Her voice said she was already tuning me out. "Okay, this is more important than your nutty inventions. Mitch, Jaden is dead."

"Jaden is dead," I repeated.

Heavy silence fell like a cloak.

'Uh, who is Jaden?"

"Mitch! Goddess save me, how can you ask me that?"

I was chewing my fingernail. When I caught myself, I frowned and stopped. Social interaction often was the stimulus for this kind of reaction. It's partly why I avoided it.

"Because I don't know who he is?"

"You had a super crush on him, remember?"

I sneezed and sneezed again. When I'd finished my fit, I tried to bring the sluggish gears in my brain around to Jaden. "I did?"

"Oh, Goddess help me," she muttered. "Keep me from being best friends with a geeky super genius who will probably invent hyperspace-capable starships but can't keep the important stuff in his head."

"Hyperspace-capable starships aren't important?"

"Jaden Ross, the gorgeous, tall, dark and dangerous guy with the motorcycle and the tats. He was killed swerving to avoid a litter of kittens on the freeway into campus."

"Oh." I decided it was better not to say it seemed like a very worthy way to go. "Are they going to name one of the kittens after him?"

EZ laughed and then she growled, as if she was pissed at me for making her laugh. I did that often, sometimes for reasons that escaped me. But I was lucky I was entertaining because she was one of my only friends. Being a freak genius inventor was on the isolating side.

"That's terrible, Mitch."

"I didn't know this guy, EZ."

"You did know him. You stared at him all the time in the cafeteria."

"I stare at a lot of people." Usually while I'm calculating elaborate math problems. It had got me in trouble sometimes. I don't know why, but people misunderstand.

"He was the one who was a ringer for Mr Darcy if he'd lived in modern times."

EZ had a major crush on Mr Darcy.

"He looked a little like the guy in the most recent *Pride and Prejudice* movie—Matthew Macfadyen."

"I liked Colin Firth's Darcy." I tried to picture Jaden. I seemed to remember a tattoo on silky golden skin hinted at through a white T-shirt. "He wore a lot of black?"

"Yes. He was a literature major. I think they have to wear black."

"Uh-huh..." I shrugged. "I'm really sorry he's dead."

She gusted out a sigh. "Me too. I thought you'd finally met someone special enough to knock you out of your lonely tower."

"I use a spare room for my experiments, *not* a tower," I said. It's why I'd rented this dumpy house. It was expensive, but I could manage it with the patents I had so far accumulated. And I needed the room.

"A spare bedroom with beeping electrodes and a weird light show."

I had to admit there was a certain Dr Frankenstein resemblance, but why fight with a classic? And all the equipment served a logical purpose.

"Well, I'm sorry the guy is dead, but I don't see why that means you have to call me nonstop," I grumbled.

EZ sighed. "Another chance at love bites the dust."

"I don't think I'm meant for love. And anyway, it's a myth. It's a molecular reaction stimulated by the impulse to procreate. In my case, that's a dead-end street."

"You could have children."

"Yes, I am capable of procreation."

"Oh, Mitch..." She sounded so depressed I searched back over the conversation to see why, but I couldn't discover the reason upon review. EZ was more complex than any equation I'd wrestled with. Most people were.

Which was why I preferred my lab and experiments. They added up.

"I have to go now." I pushed my glasses higher. I had finished washing all the dishes and wiped the counters while I was talking to her. It should be sufficient housekeeping, not counting the laundry. Oh, yeah, the laundry… I looked down at my T-shirt. Was it clean? It was wrinkled. I guess I had to do laundry as well.

"Mitch."

Ignoring EZ's attempt to continue the fruitless conversation, I cut the call. I caught myself rubbing my jaw only when I heard the rasp of whiskers. Looking out of the window, I caught my reflection in the dusty glass, a slight, hunched figure with lonely grey eyes and rumpled brown hair.

Lonely! Where did I get that? From talking to EZ.

I snorted and considered washing those windows, as if I could take away the brief vision of myself. EZ would probably say I'd had a moment with my third-eye chakra, a moment of true seeing.

I remembered the laundry. I picked up the hamper but was sidetracked when I noticed I'd written an equation on an old pair of jeans in the pile. Probably I hadn't been able to find paper and so had used the denim. The numbers seemed to blur, time fading away as I slid into the problem…

And jumped at the pounding on my door.

"I'm busy, EZ!" I called out. I knew if I let her in there would be more talk about my love life—or lack of one. I hadn't even remembered this Jaden guy until she'd brought up his death. Now I felt…like I'd missed something. I was genuinely sorry he was dead.

I growled under my breath, determined to ignore the continuous pounding. But, man, that girl had a good, strong arm.

I headed into the hallway, laundry basket on my hip.

Behind me, the front door imploded, settling with a cloud of drywall.

I dropped the laundry basket. "What the—"

"Mitchell Blake," Jaden said.

"Ah…" The silence seemed to ring, full of the fury of my door hitting the wall. My blood thudded frantically as I stared at the man who had entered my house.

Dark silky hair fell into one eyebrow. Amber-brown eyes fixed on mine. A chiselled, thin face and a full mouth.

"Jaden Ross," I whispered. "Impossible. EZ said you were—"

He stepped inside, dangerous in black leather pants, tank top and leather biker's jacket. The silver hoop in his left ear caught the light. His gaze never moved from my face.

"Mitchell," he repeated in a weirdly dead-sounding voice.

Or maybe not so weirdly. The dude was supposed to be dead!

Then I noticed Jaden's jacket was torn at the shoulder and, although his T-shirt was black, I could see a stain in the material. Blood?

Oh, come on, he's not zombie-Jaden, spared because he saved a litter of kittens.

But my throat was dry as I swallowed. "Jaden. I heard you were—" *Dead.* "Uh, that you'd been in an accident."

He cocked his head and then lifted his T-shirt. There was a dark pink line on his muscled abdomen, like the seam of a very new scar. "Accident," he repeated, in that same robo-Jaden voice.

I laughed. I sounded breathless...weak. "Okay, the door was going a bit far—did you use dynamite or something?" EZ always said it would take something like TNT to get my attention. "You're here to ask me out, right? This whole thing, her phone call, you showing up, and the zombie act, it's all an engaging way to get my attention. She knows I'm a huge science fiction geek."

Jaden continued to stare at me without speaking, without blinking. A cold chill brushed the base of my spine. And, all right, a stir of interest. He was...beautiful. Like a wild poet with that shaggy hair and those bittersweet eyes.

"Mitchell, I came for you. I will help you stay alive. Jaden liked you, trusted you."

"Enough, Jaden." His act was beginning to creep me out. Also I couldn't see any scorch marks on my door. As I knelt beside it, I saw no reason why it had suddenly flown free of its hinges and landed like a flying saucer in my hallway.

His brow crinkled. He watched me as I lifted the door from against the wall and looked on the other side. Nothing.

"All right, I'm a scientist, but I can't see how you did that trick." And I wanted to know.

"Trick?" Jaden repeated. "You did not come to the door so I removed the barrier."

"You used the power of your mind to fling it inside?" I widened my eyes at him.

"Yes."

I gusted out a sigh. "This is not funny anymore and I felt really bad when I heard you, uh, had an accident."

Jaden reached down to his left thigh, where his pants were split and spotted with dust. It looked like he'd had to lay his bike down.

"I have come for you, Mitchell Blake," he repeated. He lifted his palm and from closer up I spotted gravel and dried blood encrusted in the skin. Jesus, he'd taken a spill. "I found a form you would not find threatening." He took a step towards me and I took an automatic one back. "One you find pleasing."

"You're not Jaden." Even as I heard myself say the words I told myself I was crazy. Of course he was Jaden!

He blinked. "I can access his memories." His expression grew wooden. "Accessing…"

Get the fuck away from him! The voice came from my gut and I obeyed it, picking up the laundry basket as a pathetic weapon as I backed towards the swinging door.

"Mitchell." He frowned. "Where are you going?"

I made it into my kitchen. My BlackBerry was still on the kitchen table. I couldn't believe EZ was part of this prank. She must have been fooled into cooperating somehow. "Leave now, and I won't call the police," I said. Wow, my voice sounded cool and even, not like it wanted to shake.

Jaden had followed me, walking with a well-oiled grace. He sighed. "You are making this harder, Earthling."

Earthling. Okay, that did it. I tossed the laundry at Jaden and grabbed for my phone.

But Jaden was suddenly there, standing in front of me.

Impossible.

I looked over my shoulder to where he'd been a second ago, at the laundry scattered on the floor, then back at Jaden, into his serious brown eyes. He raised his brows, as if curious about what the Earthling would get up to next.

"I'm totally into science fiction," I said. "*War of the Worlds*, all those great black and whites with robots taking Earth women captive."

He looked like he was considering my words. "You wish me to take you captive, Mitchell?"

"What?" I flushed. "No! I'm trying to say that while calling me an 'Earthling' is just the kind of thing to make me want to go out with you, it's overkill when it comes from a guy who is supposed to be dead, who is wearing shredded clothing, and who talks about himself in the third person. Oh, and also sends my door flying." I again suppressed the spike of curiosity about how he'd done that.

Jaden reached out and took my arm. "Going out. That is a human dating ritual. It would be sufficient for my purpose."

Jaden had obviously been seriously messed up in his accident. The pink scar seemed to fade, to heal right before my eyes. I shook my head. Not possible. It was a clever trick, like my levitating front door.

"Let me go," I rasped.

He cocked his head and opened his hand, freeing me, but then he moved closer, eyes on my mouth.

I wet my lips by reflex and then rolled my eyes. Next I'd be playing with my hair in a silent, primitive signal of '*I find you hot, see how pretty I am?*' Jeez.

"Will it hurt?" His gaze lifted to capture mine.

"Hurt?" I leaned against my kitchen island, shaking like loose bones in my clothes. I could smell him, earth and pine, as if he'd caught that scent driving his bike through the morning air.

He reached out and gently cupped my cheek. His skin was hot, the palm dry and rough. "To kiss you. Will it hurt?"

"I…" I had absolutely no idea what to say. I felt like I'd been walking down a street and suddenly the pavement had given way and I'd been swallowed into a new reality.

Jaden's eyes narrowed. "Jaden thought of kissing you those times he encountered you in the cafeteria and then he hurt."

"You…thought of me?"

"It hurt," Jaden repeated, sounding vaguely accusing.

"I'm sorry." And then I noticed something, something that could not be real. As he pulled back, I saw again the back of Jaden's hand. The pink mark was now totally gone, the scar completely healed as if it had never been there. "Oh, my God… You're…" I stared into his eyes, saw an intelligence that was not Jaden, cold and fierce and assessing me. "You're really *not* Jaden."

Chapter Two

I'm not proud of what I did next. But it was not in any way my fault. The flu, the shock of Jaden's appearance, the sheer fright factor…

I fainted.

When I came to, Jaden was holding me. My head was resting against his chest and I could hear his heart beating. The scientific part of me noted his heart was beating a little too rapidly. I'd have to hook him up to one of my machines and record it. I'd have to take blood samples.

His heart's beating at least put an end to my earlier fears that he was a zombie. I mean, zombies didn't have heartbeats, did they? I didn't know for sure, since I was more into science fiction than fantasy, but it seemed a logical conclusion.

My ears were still buzzing with roaring white noise, my face warm and flushed.

My next jolt came from where we were.

I took in the giant posters I liked to look at right before I went to sleep every night and squeezed my eyes shut. No, no, no. We couldn't be in here. My bedroom, the place where my most secret self was on display.

When I dared to open my eyes and face the music, Jaden wasn't staring at the illustrations on the walls, but into my eyes, his brow furrowed. "You are not well, Mitchell. It is to be expected after your exposure to the super virus."

"Uh-huh. It's called the flu," I said. Jaden sounded pedantic...and not like the Jaden I remembered. That Jaden had been more about brooding and writing poetry, not that I'd had the chance to get to know him well.

"The virus you speak of is a catalyst," Jaden said. "It brought me here. You must not die, Mitchell."

"Not planning on it." I was blushing. Shit. I just couldn't get over that he was standing in my most private space, holding me in his arms.

"Your temperature is fluctuating." Jaden put me on my bed. When I sat up in an attempt to climb off, he shoved me back into place.

"Hey!" I croaked.

He stripped off his jacket, then took his shredded shirt in two fists and tore it from his body.

I stared. Oh, God, how could I not? I was losing my mind, I knew that, knew this had to be some weird, fever-induced episode. It couldn't be real. *He* couldn't be real.

But Jaden's smooth golden skin, now unmarred by any scars from his recent accident, was all too real. As were the black tribal-looking tattoos on the rounded muscles of his upper arms and scrawled over his pecs, emphasising the hard, smooth planes of his body. He didn't look like Mr Darcy now, but more like Tom Hardy in *Warrior.*

I wanted to lick the letters scrolled in elegant writing over his chest. I wanted to suck the ring in his left nipple into my mouth and tug it insistently with my teeth.

"You are becoming dangerously warm!" Jaden scolded. "If this continues, I'll take action to lower your temperature."

"Yeah, good luck with that." I pictured him shoving me into a cold shower. "It's not my flu," I mumbled. I was blushing even harder, if possible. Damn, I hated having such pale skin. It had made me so easy to torment in high school.

"Something is wrong."

"You took off your shirt, all right?" I growled.

He blinked then looked down at his chest blankly. Okay, there was no way he was Jaden. He looked so completely clueless as to his own attractiveness and I couldn't see Jaden being so unaware, especially with all that strategically placed ink.

"I was going to cover you with my jacket," he said.

"Very noble, but I have blankets."

He looked at the bed as if for the first time. "Your life shelf is very primitive."

"My…what?" I shook my head. I was feeling dizzy again. Crappy flu plus bad news about Jaden dying plus Jaden weirdly alive and breaking into my house and then taking off his shirt… I just wasn't up to this.

"Lie back," Jaden said gently. He knelt beside me, prodding me so I was lying flat on my back. Instantly I pictured him on top of me, inside me.

I jerked my gaze from his.

He slid a hand under my T-shirt. I gasped at his palm against my naked skin. I couldn't help how aroused I was. I could see my erection tenting my jeans, needy for his attentions.

When his hand pressed heavily into my chest, I snapped my gaze back to his face. Jaden had his eyes tightly closed. He was pale, breathing rapidly. What was going on?

Heat flashed, burning my skin where we touched. I grabbed his wrist—

"God, oh, my God!" My room lit up like an X-ray.

My eyelids lifted. I felt sleepy and warm and safe. I didn't want to move, but a wonderful feeling was edging me awake. I felt myself revolving through space and time, swirling like a dust devil, until I spiralled down into my body.

Shit. I'd fainted again?

I tensed and the arms that had been holding me set me free. I sat up, seeing I was still in my bedroom. I'd been lying against Jaden's bare chest, plastered over him.

He looked at me curiously, as if wondering what I'd do next, like I was his entertaining human pet.

I cleared my throat and then cleared it again. Something was wrong… No, something wasn't *wrong*…it was very right.

I didn't have the flu anymore.

I shoved my T-shirt up and looked at the pink handprint burnt into my skin. It was the colour of faint sunburn.

"It will fade," Jaden said, as if reassuring me. He looked vaguely uncomfortable, as if embarrassed that I bore any kind of mark.

"You…healed me," I said, even as my inner self was whispering, *not possible.*

"Of course," Jaden said. "If you are sick, it will make it difficult to go out."

"Go out?" I repeated blankly.

"With me," he said.

Oh. He meant…dating. Which struck me as the weirdest thing yet. He'd come from Goddess knew where to date *me?*

I reached out and lifted his hand. I remembered the intense heat as he'd pressed it into my chest, the feeling that he'd made contact with every cell in my body. "Who are you?" I asked.

His expression remained impassive. After a moment he said, "I am Jaden Ross."

"No, you are not." Of that, I was certain.

"He is here, parts of him. Without me, there would have been no continuing."

"You mean, he really…died," I croaked.

Jaden nodded. "In the last moments, he allowed me to take this vessel."

"Okay, that sounds monstrously complex and I'm really tempted to dive into your statement except it doesn't tell me who *you* are."

"I do not have a name, not as you do," he said, his brow crinkled.

"You don't have a name? How can you not have a name? Even a chemical formula has a name."

"I do not." He studied me. "My lack of a name concerns you."

"It does bother me," I said.

"Do not become emotional, it unsettles your matrix."

"I'll take care of my own matrix!" I yelled. Huffing, I glared at him, then realised I was being stupid. But damn. "Tell me where you come from."

"I am from another dimension of space," Jaden said simply. "I was assigned to you, Mitchell. You are the future hope of my world."

I rubbed my forehead. The flu was gone, but he was giving me a headache. "So you're…an alien."

"Yes," he said.

"I figured, with the whole 'Earthling' thing. But I guess I needed you to confirm my hypothesis. And FYI—calling me an 'Earthling' is a dorky cliché."

"I watched your television." He looked annoyed. "I researched your world. Is this body not appealing to you, not cool?"

Okay, that I couldn't deny. But he was so cute. Who was becoming emotional now? "Careful," I warned. "Your matrix is destabilising."

His eyes narrowed.

I grinned. "All right, of course you watched TV. I think it's in the 'Aliens visiting Earth for the first time' pamphlet."

"There is such a pamphlet?" Now he looked put out that he hadn't been offered one.

I laughed. "No. That was a joke."

He grunted but he didn't look amused.

"Jaden… You're inside him. So in your real form you're not corporeal?"

"I am an energy being, like you," Jaden said.

"I'm not a—Oh. You mean…my soul?" I rubbed my chest where he'd zapped me.

"Yes," he said.

"It's not very scientific, but I've always felt there was more than my physical body."

"You *glow*, Mitchell. A pure, blinding light."

"Uh, thanks." No one had ever complimented my soul before. "There's still so much I don't understand. You've come through time and space to…hook up with me?"

"I am your protector," Jaden said. "It is imperative for the people of this world and my own that you live."

"Uh-huh." I swallowed. "Am I in some kind of danger?"

"Yes," he said flatly. Then he frowned. "Mitchell, your heart rate has sped up."

"Yeah, I wonder why." I pulled my knees against my chest, pressing my head against them. I still felt kind of floaty from whatever he'd done to clear my body of the virus. "It couldn't possibly have to do with a sexy alien showing up in my kitchen, making my door implode and telling me we had to date because I'm in danger."

Jaden tugged a lock of my hair. I peeked up at him. He was looking at me quizzically. I wondered how he saw me, other than as a pretty white light. "I am sexy to you." There was a touch of smugness in his tone.

"I thought aliens were supposed to be smart," I groused. "So, yeah. You'd know I thought Jaden was—" *Hot as fuck.* "Nice looking."

"I am sorry his life path ended," Jaden said.

"Me too."

"When I mingled my essence with his in the past, I observed how he often thought of you. His energy matrix would become red and his body would hurt."

I blushed.

"I have never experienced such," Jaden continued. "Trapped inside his body, I wanted…relief."

"Yeah, that's usually what a guy wants," I muttered.

Jaden raised his brows. "I have observed lovemaking for many cycles. It looks awkward, flesh writhing against flesh, sweating bodies, hoarse cries, though the soul merging that sometimes occurs during such bonding is…" Jaden's face lit. "There are not words."

"I wouldn't know."

Jaden continued to study me.

"I don't have a boyfriend so I have no experience with the, uh, soul merging." I'd never really minded my lack of boyfriend before, despite EZ's pushing me. Usually, whenever that empty feeling pawed through my chest, I buried myself in my work.

"You wish it."

"What?"

"The soul bond." Now Jaden looked around the room, at the posters made out of book covers for the gay romance novels I illustrated in my spare time. He walked over to a recent one, where the hero, David, a New Yorker, is kidnapped by an alien, taken to his spaceship and just…taken. David's long blond hair is tangled around his naked body as he lies under a huge domineering alien warrior with purple eyes and braided black hair. The illustration features smoky pink gases that partially conceal the lovers.

"You painted this. I saw it flash into your mind when you first read the description of the story. I saw you work on it for long hours at your computer."

I dropped my gaze from Jaden's. Hardly anyone knew about my part-time job illustrating romance covers for a small press publisher. The room was covered with sketches of men kissing, touching, making love. Men in historical costumes on the verge of a forbidden embrace, men in jungle surroundings sharing a shower under a waterfall, men in cop uniforms, partially undressed as they make out. Hard bodies, faces strained on the edge of orgasm. Passion as wallpaper.

"How long have you been watching me?" I whispered.

"I have slipped into your dreams. You have very intense dreams, Mitchell."

In a flash I realised that was why I had accepted him so quickly. I knew him. He'd been inside me already.

My face heated.

Inside my mind, I scolded myself, not my body. This wasn't one of the books I illustrated. This wasn't some hot fantasy alien who was going to strip me out of my clothes and give me a whole new insight into inter-species relations.

"Why do you, uh, want to date me?"

"You have no protector," Jaden said. "I thought only to observe you, but it's clear that you need a firm hand."

"Sorry, I missed out on a protector when they were handing them out."

"Your temperature is fluctuating again, Mitchell."

"That's because you pissed me off. Look, I don't know how much you understand human beings, but I'm not looking for a 'protector'. I can protect myself just fine."

Jaden frowned. "Many of your needs are neglected. You would work better if you had a caring keeper."

I put my hands on my hips. "If you travelled light years to tell me that, you're in for a disappointment, big guy. I don't need to be kept or protected."

Jaden reached out and touched my forehead, as if to gauge my temperature. I smacked his hand away.

"The release you give yourself in the shower is not sufficient to balance out your energy matrix. I have applied myself to this problem. I can rework your pattern."

I'll just bet he could, though Goddess knew what form helping me would take. Then I realised what he'd said. "You watched me in the shower?"

He cocked his head. "I have observed all your rituals in order to understand you."

"Spying on me in the john is off limits."

"If you wish." He looked down at the grime on his body but then shrugged.

"You can use the shower," I said. "But there's a lot..." A wave of sleepiness hit me. "We need to talk about."

"You are drained from our energy blend." He guided me back to the bed. "Your matrix is aligning itself to better mingle with mine."

"We blended energy, that's how you healed me? Cool," I said groggily. I wished I was back in his arms, lying on my bed, listening to his heart pounding, feeling those long fingers stroking my hair, from scalp to ends. Oh, man, that was exactly how I loved my hair to be caressed. He might be from another star system, one I'd have to research, but he knew how to touch me.

"You have too many thoughts," Jaden said and his face looked almost indulgent. "As your protector, I will help you with that."

"Uh-huh." Back to the protector thing. I was going to have to give him hell for that. I was going to have to dig more information out of him, even though I felt like I was weighed down with everything that had happened in a very short space of time.

Jaden didn't leave me to go take his shower. Instead, he wrapped his arms around me and pulled me against the bare skin of his chest.

He held me as if he'd die to protect me.

Chapter Three

I woke up for the third time, but not in Jaden's arms. That made me cranky, which was illogical. Best case scenario, this had all been some strange dream brought on by the virus. The one I didn't have any more.

I was lying under my blankets, so I shoved them aside, lifting my T-shirt to find that yep, that hand print was still glowing faintly in the centre of my chest. I didn't have the flu, but I still had the mark Jaden had given me when he'd somehow sucked the sickness from my body.

I reached for my glasses and put them on. EZ would say I needed to meditate with each chakra—solar plexus, root, throat and third eye—in order to take stock of what was going on with my body... I didn't meditate, of course, but I did close my eyes and tune in.

I was fine. I was more than fine. I felt energised, curious about Jaden and completely lit up.

I wanted Jaden.

In the scientific sense.

I wanted to understand just who and what he was, why he was here and how his so- called powers worked. There was nothing miraculous going on here. I had to strip away all the wonder I felt, all the emotion. Then I'd be in control again. Then this would be a sequence of events I could put into perspective.

Jaden was not my fate. He was not a sexy alien who would become my lover like in the futuristic gay romances I illustrated. We were not going to have a happy ending, floating through pink clouds and making love.

Jaden was standing in my hall doorway, looking at me, his shaggy hair rippling around his face like dark water. He looked like a wild selkie, fresh out of the ocean in search of a lover he could lie with. He was naked, body glistening with moisture.

He was naked.

Jaden Ross was in my bedroom. Naked.

Definitely something was wrong with this picture.

"You have a tat on your stomach," I heard myself say. "Did that hurt more than getting one on your arm? There are a lot of nerves in that area of the body."

Jaden looked down at the sunburst that teased just above where the hair at his crotch started. He ran a finger over the black ink, as if discovering it for the first time himself. "It is newer than the others," he noted. "I was not there when it was created."

"Probably a good thing," I noted dryly.

He ran his fingers over his cock, totally unselfconsciously, as if familiarising himself with his newest toy. "I have looked forward to having one of these," he said.

I laughed. "I bet."

He was frowning. "It is very vulnerable." His palm flattened protectively over his sex.

I nodded. "Yeah, that's the second thing you learn as a guy."

"Gender. It is an ancient concept for my people."

I sat on the side of my bed and he came further into the room, pacing restlessly. I didn't mind. Watching him was like watching one of my erotic illustrations come to life. Made me feel vaguely like Pygmalion.

"How do you perpetuate your species? I mean, you have to procreate, right?"

Jaden didn't look nonplussed by my question. "We enter the bodies of beings capable of the sexual act; use their bodies to create another of our kind. But it has not happened in a long time. Most of my people are uninterested in such things." He looked into my eyes. "We have no children, Mitchell. No future."

"Uh-huh. You're different from the rest of your people, aren't you?"

"My ancestors were of a warrior line. I have tried to meditate, to be content, but I am…restless."

"Yeah." I understood him on a gut level. I wasn't a warrior, but I was restless. I was always hopping from one experiment to another, or spending my excess energy on my illustrations. Jaden came from a place I couldn't imagine. But he felt familiar.

I shook my head at the last thought. I was getting overly emotional again. I had to put a lid on that.

"My people have no interest in the sex act." Jaden sat beside me. He fell back on his elbows on the bed as if he were sunbathing, utterly oblivious to his effect on me. "They think it primitive, degrading."

I rubbed a hand through my hair, feeling how it was stiff from sleep. Great. I had my mad-scientist hair. I probably looked like a rumpled nerd sitting next to Jaden, who could have starred in his own porn movie.

"Sex can be degrading," I said. "The last time I had it, it definitely would have qualified for that definition." Oh, shit. What was I doing? I was supposed to be prodding Jaden for more information about his world, not bringing up an incident that still had the power to make me cringe.

Jaden straightened from his indolent pose. He glared at me. "Who would dare?" he demanded.

"Look, forget I said that, okay?" I laughed and it sounded forced to my own ears. "We were talking about you. That's what's important."

"I am your protector, that is all you need to know," he said.

"Obviously the alpha male also exists in your world."

"The what?" He slashed a hand in emphasis. "It is unimportant. I knew you were in danger, but I did not know that you had been abused."

My cheeks flamed. "I wasn't! I… I let myself down, all right? Now, can we let this drop?"

"I drop nothing."

"Yeah, I remember what you did to my door." I rubbed my eyes. Well, I wanted to know all about him, so it was fair he knew about me. Maybe it would be better to just get this out. I cleared my throat. "I went to a Halloween party last year. Do you know what that is, Halloween?"

"People wear masks. It is confusing." He studied me. "I looked for you but I could not find you."

"Good thing." I gusted out a breath. "Have you ever seen the movie *Carrie*? It's based on this book by Stephen King."

He shook his head.

"It's an old one now, but when I was a kid, I liked watching the first part of it. All these jerks pick on this girl in high school." And man, I wouldn't know anything about that. Sweat prickled my hairline. I could feel the walls of my school closing in around me, so I was small and lost in a hallway swirling with bigger kids. "I only watched the first part of the movie because I didn't like the second half. I kind of had…an experience recently like that." And I couldn't tell him more now. I just couldn't.

"Mitchell." Jaden put a palm on my chest, throwing me for a moment. God, he was so freaking beautiful. I stared at him, itching to trace the lines of his face, to rub a finger over his plump bottom lip. Then a strange thing happened—his hair began to shiver around his face as it took on a life of its own and his eyes lit, glowing with gold energy.

"What the—"

I felt warmth again, but it wasn't the searing heat I'd experienced when he'd healed my body. Holy crap! His energy forced its way inside me, a small molten tendril.

"*Stop!*" I smacked his hand off me.

I jerked away from him. "Back…off," I panted. "Jesus."

"I had not completed my task," he said.

"I felt you. You were inside my head." More than just my head. I'd felt him brush against my feelings, my memories.

"Your matrix—"

"I'm tired of hearing about my freakin' matrix. Stay out of my mind!"

Jaden didn't look like he was going to go along with that. Why did I have to get the alpha male alien? They were fun to read about, but in real life, not so easy to get along with.

"I would soul bond with you," Jaden rasped, his eyes still hot gold. He ignored my efforts to shove him away and pulled me firmly into his arms.

His energy matrix wasn't the only thing that was excited. His erection prodded my side. He hissed as we made contact and looked down his body. "It hurts again, Mitchell."

I was in a similar state. I didn't want him in my head again, but Jeez, there was only so much hot alien warrior I could take without touching him.

"Let me," I whispered. "Trust me."

I took his cock in my hand and watched his eyes widen. He'd watched sex, sure, but he'd obviously had no idea how good it felt to have your dick in someone's hand. I stroked him and he groaned, trembling. "Feel good?"

"No," he said, sounding vaguely alarmed. "It is uncomfortable." He touched his heavy sac.

"You're building up to feeling *very* good," I reassured him. I couldn't help it, I loved drawing this out. I could have jerked him off quickly, but then it would have been over, the magic of my hand on him.

He shut his eyes, his lips parting. I wanted to kiss that mouth. "Open your eyes," I ordered him. I needed to see him, watch him like a film.

He did as I asked, and then thrust into my hand, demanding, gearing up to take over.

So I released him.

Panting, he glared at me. "You do not stop!" he bellowed.

"I'm in charge, big guy," I told him.

"In charge?"

"Don't get pushy." He didn't look convinced. I licked my lips, as into this as he was. I was aching with arousal, but I wanted to please him. "It'll be so amazing if you let me take you there. If you just…give yourself."

He didn't take long to think about it. "Touch me as you have been doing, Mitchell. Do it now. Now!"

"All right, all right…" I muttered, but I loved that he was so needy. I curled my hand around him and Jaden had nothing to be ashamed of in the body he'd chosen. He was built solidly everywhere, though unlike me, Jaden hadn't been circumcised. It added to that wild poet thing, going perfectly with the tattoos on his chest and upper arms. "Lie back."

He blinked but then he obeyed me, since I was still giving him the stimulation he'd demanded.

The picture he made hit me again, a solid punch to the gut, just like when he'd been standing in my bedroom naked. Jaden sprawled on my floor, next to some of my clean socks that I hadn't got around to putting away yet. He looked wanton with his half-closed eyes glowing in the soft light. His body was still moist from his shower, and warm and so goddamned vulnerable, as only bare skin can be.

He moaned and rocked his hips into my caress.

I bent down and took that saucy nipple ring into my mouth, sucking and then tugging it firmly.

He shouted, bowing up as I worked his erection and teased him by tracing the graphic black lines swirling around his chest with my tongue.

"Mitchell, I am not comfortable!"

I laughed at the edge in his voice, but then I saw the fear in his eyes. Playing the voyeur hadn't prepared him for giving himself, for losing control. My throat tightened as I remembered all too well how humiliating it could be to surrender to the wrong person.

But that wouldn't happen to Jaden. I would keep him safe.

I grazed my mouth against his, feeling his breath warm against my lips. He obviously didn't know what to do, how to kiss me. I didn't push him, but stared into his eyes, watching them glaze over, the gold becoming misty.

"That's it. You're so fucking beautiful. You're safe, you know? You are so safe with me," I muttered, talking to him as I played him, bringing him closer to release. I couldn't wait to watch him come.

"Mitchell…" he groaned. His body jerked like a puppet at my every touch.

I bent over his cock and took him in my mouth.

Jaden roared, hands digging into my skull, no gentleman as he climaxed hard, shooting hot into my mouth.

I drank him, starving for his taste, starving for the desperation in his touch and the way he bucked up, shoving himself as deep as he could, his ragged breathing, his whimper when my mouth became too intense in the aftermath.

I sat back on my heels, looking down at him and…total peace. There was no other way to describe his expression now.

His big, rough biker's hands had fallen beside his head, palms up, fingers curled. His eyes were sleepy, his hair framing his face like dark lace. His olive skin was flushed from climax.

"Stay like that!" I ordered, snatching my digital camera off my desk. I snapped a couple of pictures before I realised this wasn't really cool behaviour right after what we'd done.

Jaden just watched me with lazy curiosity, innocence shining in his eyes.

"I'm taking these so I can paint you later," I said. "And I didn't think… You may not want pictures of you like this. I can delete them if you want."

Jaden's brow creased. "Why not take my picture?" he asked.

I had to grin. Yeah. If you looked like Jaden, why not? But my sexy alien didn't understand all the ramifications and I'd promised him I'd keep him safe. "Some guys might put your photo up on the internet or something," I said. "But I really only want it so I can try to paint you. I'd never show it to anyone without your permission."

"I like your paintings," he said. "I have watched you create them."

"Jaden… Thank you."

Now the gold was back in his eyes. A wicked sparkle, as if he was amused. "I thank you. You know how to service a warrior."

"Um. Thanks." I swallowed. This was getting intense. I really needed to regain my perspective. But first I had to tell him how much it meant to me, the way he'd let himself fall, the way he'd given himself to me. "You were… I don't have words. I'm better at painting. Maybe I can show you how gorgeous you are to me."

He closed his eyes. "Paint. I must recover my energy. Some parts of my matrix are still floating around this room." He yawned. "I have never felt such."

Typical guy. Now he was all about sleep. I yanked the spread off my bed and tucked it over him. I wanted to kiss him. I wanted to crawl under it with him and hold him.

"Mitchell." His voice was drowsy. "You made me a man, did you not?"

Screw it. I'd ached to be held after my first time, but what I'd got had been a nightmare. I didn't want that for Jaden. I lifted the covering and slid under it, wrapping my arms around him and enjoying his contentment despite how my own body still throbbed. "I'll keep you safe," I whispered.

I was sure he'd argue with me, bring up that protector business again, but instead he started to snore. And the stupid thing was, he was even perfect doing that.

Chapter Four

I was playing my Hapi drum when Jaden found me in my laboratory.

My hands whispered over the sensitive metal plates and notes chimed softly. "I didn't wake you?"

He was still naked. For some reason that brought home to me that this was not a normal, regular guy. I knew that even if I'd looked like Jaden I would not have had the self-confidence to walk around naked in someone else's house. I'd be too worried about whether I needed a shower or whether my hair was sticking up.

Then again, my first time had been enough to make me never want to embrace that kind of vulnerability again.

"The sound you are making moved through my body," Jaden said, which yeah, I guess meant it had woken him up.

"It's supposed to hit the different chakras," I said. "Or so EZ told me. It was a gift from her."

His brow crinkled. "Your best friend. You call her EZ."

"Yeah." I picked up one of the strikers and the water-like notes pealed from the drum, pure as church bells. Jaden sat down cross-legged beside me, looking absorbed in the music I was creating.

"You played this instrument frequently after Halloween," he noted.

Even though my belly jerked, I nodded. "Purging," I said.

"You saw to my warrior's needs."

"Yeah, I did." I had to grin at his quaint phrasing. "It was no hardship, believe me."

"But you changed the CD, Mitchell."

"I…what? I don't follow." But I think I had an idea what he was getting at…

"You did not want to talk about Halloween." He reached out and gripped my wrist, bringing my drumming to a halt. "You touched me and I forgot to make you tell me what happened to you. But I remember now."

"Couldn't I just give you another happy ending?"

"No. You said you were abused." Oh, boy, he was not giving up. His eyes had those same gold sparks and now his hair was shifting restlessly, signalling the energy crackling around him.

"I said I hurt myself…" I yanked my wrist free. "All right, you really want to know? Fine." But the words didn't miraculously spill out. I didn't want to tell him. I didn't want to tell anyone. "Not even EZ knows everything," I finally said.

His response to this was to knit our fingers together. It was such a boyfriend thing, a thing I'd never experienced. "There's a lit student named Riley Daniels," I said.

Jaden frowned. "Jaden knew him. He believes he is an amusing person, but shallow."

It was weird hearing Jaden's likes in the present tense, but also kind of comforting that a big part of him lived on.

"Yeah, Riley's a laugh a minute." I let out a breath and, nope, it wasn't getting any easier to share this. "I thought Riley…liked me," I said.

Jaden didn't blink. "Why would he not like you?"

"No, I mean, like with a capital 'L'." When Jaden still looked clueless, I tapped out a melody on my drum, avoiding his eyes. "I hadn't been with anyone. I was…in high school. I didn't want anyone to know I was gay. It was bad enough, being so geeky. So I painted out all the feelings I couldn't express in real life." I swallowed. "You saw my bedroom walls. I guess it was a useful thing, since it turned into a semi-career in illustrating romance novels."

Jaden settled in to listen to me as if I was a story teller. Somehow that made it easier.

"It was the *Carrie* scenario I mentioned before. Riley, the popular college guy, asks me out on a date. At first I can't believe it. No way is he gay. I've never seen him with another man…but he seeks me out in the cafeteria, in the library. Hell, he even goes into the science wing of the university. I was sure, if he went that far, he had to be for real." I wished I could go back in time, have a seriously grounded in reality talk with my more innocent self. "So I finally agree to go out with him to a party on campus." I licked my lips. My throat was burning. "I need some water."

There was a little popping sound and a mug full of water appeared beside my drum. I jumped. "Holy shit!"

That humour glinted gold in his eyes. "You said you wanted water."

I picked up the mug cautiously, took a sip. Regular H_2O from the taste. "I'm going to want to understand how you do that," I said. "Scientifically."

Jaden nodded. "Of course."

"Okay, good." I took a gulp, but then couldn't put it off any longer. "I was a wreck. I'd never gone to a college party before. Just little coffee get-togethers with EZ and her friends. I knew I'd need help, so I told her about Riley. At first she was like me, sceptical, but…but I talked her into believing he had a thing for me. I think, looking back, I was also talking myself into it."

"This was how you…allowed yourself to be harmed?" Jaden prodded. But he picked up the mug, shoved it at me so I could swallow some more water. If I didn't know better, I'd say he was actually worried about me.

"Yeah, it is. I didn't hang out with Riley's crowd. Frankly, they scared the shit out of me. I was great at science, math, living in my own head, but I wasn't good with people. I'm still not so great."

"You have EZ," Jaden said.

I drank the last of the water. "Thank Christ. Anyway, Riley's crowd…they were the factor I hadn't let myself consider in the equation. He wasn't dating me, he was courting *them*."

"Your date was a trap."

I nodded. "I got all dressed up. I blew a month's rent on a cashmere sweater. I got my hair cut in this salon that EZ said was the place. I looked good. For me, I mean."

"Why would you not look good? You look good to me now."

My face heated at the way he was looking at me. He was not complimenting me. To him, he was stating a fact. And it was nice. "Thanks. But I just wanted to say that, for the record, I looked as good as I'm capable of looking."

I fiddled with the drum strikers. "I got to his place and I was earlier than he'd expected. His parents are fronting his education so he can afford to live in his own apartment and it was full of books. When I saw some of EZ's early ones, I thought, here it is—the smoking gun."

"I am lost," Jaden said.

"EZ writes romances, sometimes gay romance. She's self-pubbed a few titles and I illustrated them. Anyway, finding them at Riley's was a sign. No way a straight guy would have those books."

Jaden still looked a little befuddled, so I told myself not to rush. He really wanted to hear this and suddenly I wanted to tell him. "Riley made me an espresso and his kitchen was small and we bumped and…we made out in his kitchen. It was my first time with anyone. I was too hot to be nervous and I got the feeling he felt the same way." I laughed. "It was so perfect I even had this Madonna soundtrack running through my head, all her early songs. Then…we went to the party."

Jaden pulled me closer so I was sitting on his lap. "That's when the joke factor entered the picture. Everyone else was dressed up, but I didn't know it was that kind of party. Then I found out he'd been dared to bring a guy as his date by his fraternity. I was so dumb I didn't even know he belonged to one. I, uh, found out about the big gag when his girlfriend showed up. Everyone was in on it except me."

"This is terrible!" Jaden muttered.

"Yeah." I cleared my throat. "The worst part was I didn't know how to act. I needed to get out of there without showing how upset I was. I pretended I'd been in on it. When I was leaving, Riley looked at me for the first time since we'd done it at his place. His eyes… He was living a lie."

Jaden ran a finger over my cheekbone and down to my chin. "You are *not* living a lie."

"No," I said and I'd never been happier about that than I was as he pressed his closed lips clumsily against mine.

"Mitchell, you-hoooo! Are you home?"

"That's EZ," I told Jaden. "She has a key, though I guess that's moot because my door is toast." And somehow, with everything going on, I'd forgotten the door. I was going to have to rig something up.

I heard EZ clunking up the stairs and then she was framed in the doorway, tiny, with long brown hair and the tattoo of a butterfly on her exposed collarbone. She looked at me and then Jaden, whom I'd just remembered was completely naked.

"Mitchell… Oh, my God, what have you done!" she screeched.

"I didn't raise him from the dead in one of my experiments, EZ," I said dryly.

She opened her mouth, closed it. "But he's…"

Oh, shit. How was I going to explain Jaden?

Jaden got up, all lean build and silky olive skin. He held out his hand to EZ. "You are Mitchell's friend."

"Um, yeah. Looks like so are you!" she said. "I'm glad you're not dead." She glared at me and I knew she was wondering why I hadn't told her that Jaden was my special naked friend. "Mitch," she continued. "What the hell happened to your front door?"

"I was working on something," I said, which wasn't altogether a lie. I had been planning on working on something when Jaden had blasted his way into my house.

EZ grimaced. "Why am I not surprised? And I'm seriously interrupting..." She didn't blush as she began to retreat, instead checking Jaden out thoroughly. I couldn't blame her.

"Wait!" I couldn't do it. I had no idea how I was going to explain everything, but I couldn't leave EZ in the dark. She could be a pain in the ass, but she had always, always wanted me to be happy. She was my only family, since the aunt and uncle who'd raised me had been distant and done it only out of obligation. "EZ, Jaden is an alien."

EZ blinked. "Like, from Mexico or something?" She gave Jaden a sympathetic look tinged with lust. "That must be tough. I never would have guessed."

"No," I sighed. "Jaden, go get some clothes on." No way was EZ going to be able to pay attention with Jaden's gorgeous body on display.

Jaden frowned. "You and I have much to discuss."

"I'm not going anywhere. Just..." I got up, went to him. Looking into his eyes, touching that tangled hair, I couldn't believe I hadn't been as distracted as EZ was now when I'd talked to him earlier. But it had been about comfort, about...intimacy maybe. I had never experienced it, but I thought that was the best word for what we'd shared.

"I know you probably don't understand, but nudity is kind of a big deal."

"My clothes are damaged and soiled."

"Borrow whatever of mine will fit you."

"You will be here when I have dressed myself?"

"Yeah."

As soon as he disappeared, EZ hissed, "So, I guess it was a fun joke to pretend you didn't know Jaden."

"I didn't…" I lifted a hand to hold off an explosion. "Listen, I'm going to tell you everything and you're going to think I'm crazy."

"Uh-huh." She still looked hurt.

"I didn't know Jaden," I told her. "Not until he broke through my door this morning."

"He broke your door?"

So I told her everything. She looked incredulous and I flushed, knowing how it sounded. Then I just waited.

Jaden returned wearing a T-shirt with a Hawaiian flower lei scrawled across the chest. It was tight enough to hug his pecs. It was also wrinkled, since I'd never finished sorting through my laundry, but I think it was clean. He'd snagged some shorts to go with it. My jeans were probably too tight on him.

He looked at EZ. "Mitchell says I shouldn't call you an Earthling. He says it's a cliché."

EZ laughed. "Is he for real?" she asked me.

And just like that she was floating three inches off the floor. Her hair hung down, brushing the hardwood. *"Oh, my Goddess!"*

Jaden merely looked on, serenely.

Then I was floating beside EZ. Like one of those happy dreams you have about flying, like anything is possible. I'd left some of the dark, smudgy stuff from Halloween behind me by opening up to Jaden, so it seemed fitting that suddenly I was weightless.

EZ grabbed my arms. "Mitchell, you're not doing this! This is not one of your lame attempts to create anti-gravity."

"Nope," I said. "This is Jaden."

Chapter Five

Something loosened in my chest when Jaden suddenly floated up beside us, all three of us bobbing above the floor. My sexy alien had a goofy side.

"This is so much fun!" EZ yelled, giggling madly. I laughed with her, maniac best friend laughter as we rolled like puppies in free fall. Jaden watched us and a tiny, awkward smile touched his lips.

EZ reached out and yanked Jaden closer, into our circle. As soon as she did that, we smacked into the floor. My sides were hurting from laughing so hard.

Jaden looked embarrassed. "You made me lose my concentration," he told EZ, looking mildly annoyed.

"Please," EZ said. "Guys always blame the woman for that."

I grinned when poor Jaden only looked confused.

EZ's head was pillowed on my stomach. I threaded fingers through her hair, stroking it. Jaden's eyes narrowed as he watched us. If I didn't know better, I'd say he was pouting.

"So, can you, like, take Mitchell flying?" EZ asked in a dreamy voice. "Like Superman and Lois Lane?"

"You want to fly?" Jaden asked me.

I laughed again. "Well, yeah, who wouldn't? But I've always envisioned doing that with an anti-gravity device of some kind." I frowned as I considered my theories.

"I can take you flying," Jaden said. "But we have to be…discreet."

"Because you're an alien."

"Because I am not the only one of my kind here, Mitchell," he said, very seriously.

EZ sat up, hair swinging so it hit my face. I shoved the stuff away and concentrated on Jaden. The rigid way he was sitting was cueing me into the realisation that another of Jaden's friends being here was not a good thing.

"You said I was in danger. That you'd come here to be my…protector." EZ shot me a look and I flushed. Damn it, I was just repeating what Jaden had told me. It wasn't like I was signing on to give Jaden my balls and stop taking care of myself.

"The previous attack was on Halloween," Jaden said.

"Riley?" My voice gave an embarrassing crack. "He's an evil alien out to do me in?"

Jaden shook his head. "Not Riley, but when I mapped the illness in your matrix it originated from that time."

"Yeah…" I had been sick since Halloween. It was December now and I'd had this bug on and off for weeks. "I haven't been able to shake this thing."

"You even went to the university clinic for antibiotics after I nagged you about it," EZ put in, frowning.

"You're saying there was more to my flu than…the flu?" I wasn't scared, I was fascinated.

EZ rolled her eyes. "You're a victim of possible germ warfare and you're enraptured by the scientific possibilities. Typical Mitchell."

Jaden nodded. "When I realised you had been ill too long, I had to pour myself into a body so I could speak with you, heal you."

"So when Jaden had his accident this morning it was convenient."

"Yes, but also for Jaden. Now his human matrix lives on with me. It was an agreeable arrangement for both of us," Jaden said.

"If Riley didn't give me some kind of sleeper bug, who did?"

"It could have been anyone at that party you attended, a person taken over by my opponent."

I blinked. This was hard to take in. I'd had a crappy romantic experience, but it turned out it could have been a fatal one.

I could have died.

"Why?" I asked.

"Why does my opponent want you dead?"

"Yeah, and let's call him Mr X," I said. "Just easier to give him a name."

Jaden spread his hands. "I told you that you are important to two worlds. In the future, your inventions make it possible for many of my people to become corporeal again if they choose. In return for your technology, we will make contact with Earth, gift your people with cures to diseases, advances in sciences. But you are the key, Mitchell. If you aren't allowed to grow and develop your gift, it will never happen and our worlds will remain separate, to the detriment of us both."

"So this Mr X isn't down with the idea of having a body again?"

Jaden nodded. "He believes we are pure as we are, as energy alone. To live in flesh is to degrade our purity."

"He sounds like a fanatic," EZ said. "We have a few of those here on Earth."

"So, at the Halloween party, he could have been anyone," I mulled, trying to get a handle on the situation.

"Yes."

"But you didn't do what he did, just take someone over. I mean, you said you've been inside me and Jaden in the past, but I wasn't aware of you."

"It is unethical to take over another being," Jaden said stiffly. "I wanted to know you, but to truly merge I'd need your permission. You haven't granted it."

I remembered how I'd swatted him when he'd tried some kind of soul cleanse. "No, I haven't, but obviously Mr X doesn't care about asking for permission."

"So he's like…a creepy shape-shifter!" EZ exclaimed, leaping on the point I'd been about to make.

"Yes, although I take issue with creepy. *I* am not creepy," Jaden said stiffly. "Jaden agreed to our merging. He is braided to my consciousness."

"Symbiosis," I said.

"Two for one," EZ said with a smirk. "Hot alien warrior and brooding biker poet all in one very cute body."

"I am cute?" Jaden asked. Then, before EZ could restate the obvious, he repeated smugly, "I am cute. I am a cute human."

"A cute guy," EZ coached.

"A cute guy."

"Can we please focus here? We have a shape-shifting fanatical alien on the loose whose goal is to give me the super flu…and, hello, that's kind of odd, now I think of it," I said. "Why not just run me over with a car?"

But Jaden was shaking his head. "He has to be subtle. There are factions among my people. If you die what appears to be a natural death, then he can't be accused of interference."

"Wow, I guess, despite being pure energy beings, you haven't left politics behind," EZ said.

"We have more time for debate since we lack physical bodies."

"I guess so, if you can't even have sex."

"Mitchell aided me in experiencing my first climax," Jaden told her earnestly. "It was very satisfactory. I want him to give me more orgasms very soon."

"Um…huh." EZ's expression was a little too bland. "How nice of Mitchell."

My cheeks burned. "Jaden, you don't announce stuff like that. It's…private."

"Don't listen to him," EZ said. "You can tell me all about it. Anytime. And if you have pictures, that's a bonus."

"EZ! He doesn't know you're joking."

"Hell, who's joking?"

Desperately, I brought us back on topic. "So now you've healed me, Jaden, won't the alien assassin try again?"

Jaden nodded. "Even I can't know what face he will wear, not until he attempts to harm you again."

"Comforting."

"I am your protector. You must submit yourself to me."

"I'd rather be your partner," I said. "I'm not stupid. I know I need help, but I'm at a critical point with two of my experiments and I have to be on campus to monitor one of them."

"I must stay with you. Now I have merged with Jaden, I cannot easily leave this body."

"Why would you want to?" EZ muttered, but Jaden and I ignored her comment.

"Okay..." I rubbed my jaw and remembered I had yet to shave, but now I felt like I had the energy to take better care of myself, since that low grade flu was gone. "So maybe Mr X has that same problem of jumping easily into another body, Jaden. He could be in the same one he used on Halloween." I looked at EZ. "Since you're the social butterfly on campus, I need you to try to remember who was at the frat party," I said. "Maybe we can narrow down anyone who might be our guy."

"Right, take note if anyone at the party has been acting strange. I'm on it. Why don't we meet tomorrow for coffee in the science library?" she said, getting to her feet and stretching. "I have to teach a restorative yoga class in half an hour, so I've got to get going anyway."

"I would like to take yoga," Jaden said wistfully. "From what I've observed it has a very interesting effect on the human nervous system."

"Jaden, you may be the perfect man."

Jaden beamed at her. I raised a hand. "Hang on, I have done yoga. It just didn't do anything for me."

Jaden was looking at me with the singular attention of a dog wanting to be fed and I realised that yoga would certainly be a powerful way of experiencing his new body. "All right, but I need a shower and shave first. And I'm not going to twist myself into downward bunny or whatever."

"It's downward dog, Mitchell," EZ said. She put an arm around Jaden as his face lit.

My belly twisted, looking at him. So much innocence on that narrow, poet's face.

On impulse I pressed my mouth to his. When I would have pulled away, Jaden stopped me. "Mitchell…" he growled, looking at my lips. "You move me."

My Beloved Yoga was on the edge of the university, right before woods sprouted, surrounding the campus in Douglas firs and red cedars. EZ's mother owned the studio, so EZ had grown up drinking wheat grass juice served in the adjacent organic cafe and doing headstands when her mother wasn't packing her off to India on pilgrimage. I figured EZ'd end up taking over the business one day, but in the meantime she attended various women's studies classes, which usually left her pissed off and hating all men. I was the exception since being gay didn't make me as much of an oppressive pig in her eyes.

I'd managed to dig up sweatpants for me and Jaden. It wasn't cool and expensive yoga wear, but it would do. Before we'd left my house, Jaden had repaired the front door. EZ and I had watched goggle-eyed as he'd levitated it back into place and then fixed the damage with a casual wave.

Now Jaden was practically vibrating with excitement as he paced the studio space, looking at posters of the chakra symbols and studying the display of Tibetan singing bowls and rose quartz candle votives.

"Just take it easy today, Jaden," EZ advised him as people began to arrive for her laid-back class. "Remember to listen to your own body."

"My own body…" he repeated. "I have a body!"

I rolled my eyes and sat down on one of the mats, noting that EZ didn't spare much advice on me. But she knew I was hopelessly unathletic and usually spaced out into thinking about my work when I did asanas. I just couldn't concentrate on my breathing when I might be on the verge of solving a problem.

Jaden was attracting attention. At first I thought it was merely his incredible good looks, those brown eyes that could glow an uncanny gold and the flowing hair he'd tied back, but then I remembered he'd been featured in the news.

He was supposed to be dead.

Well, this was awkward.

But we'd figure out a cover story; that the reporter had got the name wrong. It should work in the short term. And then it hit me. Okay, he'd told me he'd taken over Jaden's body in a hurry when he'd realised something was wrong with me, that I wasn't getting over my flu. Did he mean to stay Jaden after we'd dealt with Mr X? Or would he have to leave, to return to his people?

Maybe he was extra eager to experience things like yoga and climaxes because it was a one-time deal.

"Mitchell, you are not concentrating on your breathing," Jaden scolded me.

"How do you know?"

"Your matrix."

"Right. Shoulda known." I closed my eyes and tried to pay attention to my chest rising and falling instead of Jaden leaving my life as abruptly as he'd entered it.

Yoga class turned out to be not so bad. Apparently, restorative involved a lot of lounging around in weird positions on cushions and yeah, more breathing. I did tune out sometimes to consider my current projects, but every time I did, Jaden knew and prodded me to refocus on the class.

"You are as important as your work, are you not?" he demanded.

I was more comfortable in the cafe, sipping espresso served by EZ's mom. Sitting with EZ and Jaden felt like I was with my two best friends. If life could always be like this…it would be perfect. Better than the fake relationship I'd gone for at the Halloween party.

And speaking of fake relationships, who should walk in right then but Riley and his girlfriend.

Perfect.

EZ caught my tension and looked over her shoulder. "Those French braids aren't very attractive on Mallory," she said, referring to Riley's blonde girlfriend, Mallory Clark. "Her hair isn't long enough." EZ's hair, in contrast, was long enough to look great in French braids.

"It's okay, EZ," I told my friend. "I've seen him around a few times since Halloween. No big deal."

But Jaden's eyes were narrowed and his hair stirred, even though there was no breeze in the cafe.

"Jaden…" I gripped the back of his hand.

"Mitchell." I looked up and there was Riley, rubbing the back of his neck, body language awkward. He didn't meet my gaze, but instead focused on my hand covering Jaden's. I tried to yank it away, but Jaden snagged it firmly.

Riley flushed, cleared his throat. "I was wondering if you could help me out with an assignment I have in geology," he said. "I know it's not precisely your thing, but it's still science, right?" He gave one of his easy, flirtatious smiles.

"He can't," EZ said flatly.

"EZ," I admonished her. Why did she and Jaden automatically assume I needed protection? I swallowed, looking at Riley. I could still feel his hands tracing my arms, feel his mouth sucking on my nipple.

His eyes flashed with heat and I realised he was remembering the same thing.

"Mitchell will not give you another climax," Jaden said. "Ever."

Breath gusted out of Riley's chest as if Jaden had just hit him in the gut. He'd cut through all the bullshit to the real reason Riley had come to our table.

"What the fuck!" Riley's face was red and sweating. Not attractive.

Jaden still gripped my hand. His expression was serene.

"So you got a new boyfriend now," he hissed at me, quietly enough so no one beyond our table—including his girlfriend—could overhear.

"Yes," Jaden said, at the exact time I said 'uh'.

"Mitchell is under my protection," Jaden continued.

"Didn't know you were into kinky shit," Riley said, giving me a scathing glance. It was surreal. I was just…Mitchell. Boring, thin-shouldered science nerd. But Jaden and Riley were acting like I was a hot commodity.

"I'm not kinky. I mean…I don't know if I am." I was babbling. I sucked in a deep breath. "I'm not into you anymore, Riley."

"Your loss!" Riley whispered hotly. Then he was striding back to his table and I knew I'd ceased to exist for him.

"What a jerk face," EZ said. "Like you're so needy you'd meet him behind his girlfriend's back."

"I would never have done that," I said. And it felt good to recognise that.

"He can't have your energy matrix," Jaden said, still glaring after Riley. "It is mine."

Chapter Six

I paced the science library I staked out every Thursday. It had been built in the early twentieth century, so it was full of fanciful turrets, stained glass windows and even the odd gargoyle. Usually the setting amused me, seemingly so untouched by Darwin, but today I couldn't settle down to one of my projects. I was restless, jittery. Pissed off.

Hunched over the scarred maple table near the window overlooking campus, Jaden flipped through an old issue of *Scientific American.*

"How can you be so Zen about everything?" I demanded.

Jaden looked at me. Blinked. "Zen?"

"Yeah, Zen. Like some alien assassin stalking me is no big deal."

"It is a very big deal, Mitchell, or I would not be with you now, in this body," Jaden said. But a hint of gold glittered in his eyes. He wasn't as calm as he seemed.

I gritted my teeth to stop myself from snapping at him.

"I wouldn't have slept with him again," I said. "Riley, I mean."

"No, I wouldn't have allowed it."

"No, you mean *I* wouldn't have allowed it."

"Your energy matrix is dangerously unstable."

"My energy matrix, my problem."

"So it is." He went back to his magazine.

"Look, I think we need to get a better handle on the problem with Mr X."

He shoved the magazine aside and crossed his arms. The way he was slouching and the slightly sulky pout to his mouth reminded me that part of him was the poet, the English major. It also made it clear that I wasn't the only one on edge.

"Are you going to keep taking classes here?" I asked, then looked away, unable to hold his gaze. Boy, what an obvious fishing expedition. I might as well have asked how long he intended to stay with me.

"I…don't know." Jaden chewed his lip. "I find the idea strangely appealing. I haven't had enough time to study your literature. But it is not my primary mission."

"Yeah, great," I mumbled. Was that a 'yes, I'm staying to finish my degree' or a 'no, I'll be gone on the next full moon'? Couldn't he be clear? And now I was pouting.

"Mitchell, I cannot read your mind unless you allow the soul bond."

"No way." It would be just too embarrassing for him to get a look at how pathetic I was feeling.

"Fine. Perhaps I can go back to my reading?" He raised his brows, very cool and polite.

"What's eating you?"

"Riley is an amusing companion."

"Excuse me?" I was thrown by this tangent.

"His girlfriend was laughing while they sat together. He is charming."

I lifted a shoulder. "I guess..."

"You found him charming or you would not have gone out with him."

"He is very persuasive," I agreed.

"You thought about him. I saw the red colour of your aura when he spoke to you. You thought about how he touched you."

"I did?" I remembered that split second of connection Riley and I had shared, when I'd remembered his hands on me, his mouth. "I guess I did. It's, uh, natural with your first lover."

Jaden glowered at me, like a gothic hero from one of EZ's books.

And I got it. "You've never been jealous before. Wow."

"Wow?"

"Wait, don't get mad. Look, it's like you visited Jaden's body briefly and couldn't interpret sexual frustration so it came across as painful."

"It is painful!"

"Yeah, I guess it is. Sorry. But jealousy is like your first experience with sex. It's a powerful emotion. I'm guessing you're not used to channelling that kind of feeling. Not if your people spend a lot of time floating around debating. So this is all new to you. Overwhelming."

Jaden's hands curled into fists. "When I remember that look you exchanged with Riley, I do not feel Zen." His chest rose and fell sharply. Shit, he was in real distress.

I grabbed the chair next to him and took his arm. "I don't respect him so there's no way there could be anything between us."

"You were still aroused by him."

I rubbed my forehead. "You know, it occurs to me that most adults deal with their emotions by suppressing them and putting them aside. I didn't know what I was feeling about him…except maybe exposed. Like he hurt me again."

"Because you remembered desiring him and that opened you to him again."

"Yeah." I squeezed Jaden's hand. "Thanks. I couldn't get a handle on my bad mood until you brought it down to basics. When I remembered wanting him, I remembered how he'd hurt me. And it hurt my pride when he dismissed me after I turned down his generous offer to fuck me behind everyone's back. Stupid…"

"He was your first," Jaden said. "You are my first. You can hurt me."

"I don't want that, but I might do it." I shrugged. "I'm human."

He let out a long breath. "I don't understand the way humans communicate. You say things and sometimes it is sarcasm, but it sounds true to me. And sometimes it is not at all what you feel." He rubbed his chest.

I gave into impulse and leaned close, pressed my lips to his chest, right over his heart. "I'm sorry I made you feel insecure and angry."

"Mitchell…" he breathed.

"Tell me what you feel. You don't have to put it aside. I don't need you to pretty things up for me or wear a mask. Not ever."

"I want you to be mine the way he made you his," Jaden growled. "I want you to need me and to hold onto me, and to dig your hands in my back."

Sweat broke out on my hairline. I could feel my blood throbbing in my cock.

This part of the library was pretty secluded, but not secluded enough that someone might not come up here. I grabbed his hand. "Come on!"

"Mitchell…"

"It's okay." I kissed him again, taking a moment to use my tongue to rub his sulky lower lip. Oh yeah, he liked that. His hair was stirring and his eyes glowing. "I'll give you what you need."

"I need you, Mitchell."

His words wiped away the lingering bruise Riley had left on my psyche. "Follow me." I pulled him through dusty stacks of books to a door almost hidden by the hulk of shelving. I took out my key chain and opened it, and then we were running up a rusty spiral staircase. When we reached the top, I pushed open the second door and suddenly we were surrounded by the misty day.

"The clock tower," he said. "I've seen it from the walkways on campus, but I didn't know it was here."

"No one ever comes up here. I managed to get a key when I started teaching part-time," I said. I knelt and he mimicked my movement, completely with me. "We can touch…" I ran a finger down his arm. He pulled back, yanked off his T-shirt. "I want your hand on me." He frowned. "For some reason, I want it on my bare skin. It is imperative."

I grinned at his confusion. "Probably your reptile brain. Very primal."

"This touching is what some of my people find degrading." But he didn't look like he thought so. His eyes flared as I leaned close and took the nipple with its silver ring into my mouth. "Mitchell!"

"This is like a dream," I muttered against the taste of him, the feel of him. My hands dug into the hard round shape of his upper arms. I traced the swirls of letters banding his upper chest like a garland. *"Between two worlds life hovers like a star."*

He hissed in a breath as I took my time, savouring him. "The words of Lord Byron."

"Very appropriate for you, Jaden." I could feel his heart thundering under my lips. As I kissed him, unable to pull myself away even to undress myself, he cupped me, stroking me through my pants. "Ohhhh, Jesus."

"My scientist," he whispered. "You are irresistible. You drew me. I had to come to your world. I had to know your mind."

"You're…going to know a hell of a lot more than my mind in a moment."

He smiled. Still rusty, as if he wasn't sure what he was doing.

"You want charming? Riley has nothing on you. Your smile is charming."

He fell back at my push, lying on the floorboards that surrounded the sleeping clock works.

"You…respect me, Mitchell?" He was nude. I'd stripped him in record time, the baggy sweats no defence against my ardour. I pushed his thighs open and put my mouth on him.

"Yeah, I'll respect you in the morning, don't worry."

"You are making a joke."

He moaned and his flesh was suddenly too hot, so I jerked back in surprise.

"What's happening to you?"

His skin was glowing, translucent. I could see the blue veins like pumping highways. I could see long bones and muscles and the workings of his body as if he were a mechanical device.

"Wow," I said.

"I am undone."

I was doing this to him, making him lose control. "You're a miracle."

He didn't look convinced. "I am not pleasing to your eyes this way. I studied *Men's Health.*"

I flushed because I regularly flipped through that magazine and not because I was looking for tips on working out. "Hey, to a science nerd like me, you are gorgeous. I can see your heart actually pumping!" I saw the red pulse, the blood shooting, feeding his body with oxygen; I saw the filigree of veins in his lungs, complex as a lace pattern.

He closed his eyes tightly, let his head fall back. "It is hard with you. I ache to merge."

"I ache to merge too." I tugged at his hair and he raised his head. I could see parts of his skull through his skin, sparks of the workings of his brain. "Holy shit! You're so sexy."

"I am not."

"You kidding? I never appreciated how a man is put together until you made me see it. Before I met you it was all on the surface."

His eyes were dilated. He pulled me to him. "Mitchell, come inside me."

I blinked.

"Inside my matrix. You will not let me into yours, but I need to touch you, to truly make contact with you."

My heart pounded. "I don't have the protocol for that kind of…experiment."

"You're frightened. I have frightened you."

"You terrify me. This thing with us isn't like your typical campus romance and anyway, I've proven once I suck at those." I twisted my lips in a dry smile. My skin felt too tight and my breath hitched. "I thought we'd just come up here and fool around."

"I am not pleasing to you." He let me go. And I couldn't stand it. Couldn't stand that he would think simply because he was different I'd be repulsed.

Anger burned and I gripped his face, my fingers biting into the flesh.

He panted, staring at me and suddenly I was inside him. I was pulsing with his blood, riding the heat of life through ash coloured tunnels of bone, pitted like craters on the moon. I was a spark sliding silently through his body.

"Mitchell…" I heard him. "Let me in. It can be more than this, more than flesh. Let me show you."

I was small and frightened but I was contained. I was safe this way, with my walls around me. Even here, surrounded by the magnificent flesh of Jaden's body, I was still grounded in blood and bone and flesh.

But then I felt a whisper of loneliness. Jaden hadn't had a name until he'd come here. He hadn't known he wanted a name. He hadn't known desire or pain or jealousy or hunger until I'd awakened him.

And then, as if he'd set me free, I was back in my own body again, lying on the floor. My chest expanded like a giant balloon as I sucked in breath. My vision was blurry, my own body feeling oxygen deprived.

"Mitchell, you are in distress!" Jaden touched me. Gold sparks hit my body like tiny meteorites, penetrating my skin.

I twisted under the onslaught, unable to deal with the building energy. I shoved down my pants and took my cock in my hand, stroking my sensitised skin, my balls tight against my body, my thighs trembling as my body bowed off the wooden planks.

Streams of white light burned from my fingertips, poured from the soles of my feet and the centre of my chest and the palms of my hands.

"Jaden…" I croaked.

"Trust me." He buried his face against my neck and he was the only cool, safe place as my body erupted, as I felt the gentle brush of his energy matrix against mine.

I came, hot and scalding, clawing at his back and then I came again, writhing on the floor. "No, can't—" I choked. But I spilled again and again, my body jerking.

My hand was fisted tightly in Jaden's hair. We were tangled together, him on top of me. He pulled away to look at me with soft, concerned and very human eyes.

"What the hell was that?" I asked.

"I think…" He chewed his lip. "I think that was sex."

I groaned, shifting free so I could curl into the foetal position. My whole body throbbed, intensely alive. The air felt like hail, hurting my skin. My cock was still erect, covered with spend. I'd come so often that the last couple of times I'd been dry. It had been the most pleasurable agony I'd ever experienced.

It shouldn't have been possible.

"I will take away your discomfort," he said and he again put his palm in the centre of my chest. My stressed body soaked in his power until I felt only limp and gloriously relaxed.

Dazed, I could only watch as Jaden slipped down my body and licked me. He was trembling.

"I'm all right," I mumbled. "Just…wow."

"I did not know it would be like that."

"Uh-huh." I could barely think. His licking was beginning to feel good. He held my balls in one hand, gently, while he nuzzled my prick. He explored me, laving the rim of my cock, dipping his tongue into the tiny slit until I gasped.

"I think we need to work on merging."

"Yeah." I'd be a car wreck if we made out like that again. But just thinking of the incredible experience made me hard as stone. "Jaden, don't tease me," I begged.

So he lifted me onto his lap. I wrapped my legs around him, sagging, still limp. He held his cock against my opening. "Shhhh, I will make you ready," he comforted me.

I don't know what he had done, but I was relaxed and slippery inside. It still wasn't easy to take him, but he didn't give me a choice. He wanted in. Now.

I moaned as he pressed firmly.

"Some of my people like the idea of taking human pets," he whispered. "Of pleasuring them and keeping them."

"Take me," I whispered, lost to my dark, slutty side. "Keep me."

Chapter Seven

"Do you really want me to keep you or are your words sarcasm?" Jaden demanded, eyes burning into mine.

"Sarcasm?" I laughed and then my eyes crossed as he did something with his hips. "Can we talk about this…uh…after?"

Jaden smacked my butt. It shouldn't have felt so good. Maybe I was kinky.

"Jaden, I've never been possessed like this. I can't breathe without feeling you inside me," I said. Not just my body, but my heart. But that was so unscientific, so…vulnerable. No way could I tell him that.

"You give me more than you did that Riley person." His hands were firm on my body. "You are mine, Mitchell?"

"Yes," I whispered. I nipped his ear and he grunted as he pushed me down to take more. I was right on the edge.

"I would keep you like this for a long time."

"No, please." I didn't think I could take that. I was ready to explode like a star.

"I like the way you hold onto me, the way you beg."

"That's because you're a big, bossy alien."

He lifted me up and we both groaned as I rode him. He was so strong, unnaturally strong, so that I felt the reality of being his pet.

"Don't ever stop…"

He pressed his lips to mine, still clumsy, but warm. "I never knew flesh could feel so…" He leaned his forehead against mine. We shared breath, panting hotly. Every pulse of his hips took him deeper. My body was screaming to come, but I didn't want it to be over.

"Jaden." I pressed a kiss against the letters on his chest.

"Come for me, pet," he ordered.

It should have been eclipsed by the previous merging. This was just him and me. His hand knotting itself to mine. His eyes holding mine. His lips brushing mine, whispering encouragement so I fell, coming for him, holding on to him.

His body arched, my palm against the thunder of his heart. He cried out, the almost-pain of orgasm knotting his brow, twisting his face.

I fell against him and we were wrecked together.

"Mitchell."

"Uh." I cracked open my eyes to see the light had silvered to the colour of driftwood. It was only around three-thirty, but it was dusk already.

The parts of me not covered by Jaden's bigger body were chilled. I curled my feet and hooked them under his calves. He grunted in response, lifted himself up so he could look down at my face.

"You're squishing the Earthling," I said.

"By my calculations the clock will begin to gong soon," Jaden said.

"Um, yeah." I licked my lips but couldn't get too worked up by the idea. What had he said? Something about the clock…

And then it was ringing and the sound was like the end of the world. I shouted and covered my ears and Jaden's lips curved as he pulled me close as if to protect me. The clock tower had been revamped in the seventies. It was as musical as a blast from a car horn.

"We survived," I said, reaching for my cold, damp, crumpled sweats. Jaden had his T-shirt back on and was searching for his own workout pants, his taut, flexing rear end facing me so enticingly I had to give it a squeeze. He raised his brows over his shoulder at me.

"Sorry. It was just asking me to pinch it."

"I am a cute guy with a cute butt."

"Yeah!" I laughed. "You learn fast."

He smirked at me and I liked the confidence our lovemaking had given him. Well, not just him if I were honest about it. The thing with Riley had convinced me to put sex aside, but Jaden had changed that.

"Your energy matrix is sleepy."

"Yeah." Sleepy and pretty damn content. "I have to check on one of my experiments."

"I will wait. EZ gave me one of her books to read."

"Really?" I wasn't sure if that was a good or bad thing. My best girl wrote some pretty stimulating love scenes.

We clanged down the steps and skulked back into the main library. Jaden didn't want to leave me alone in my lab so he came with me and read while I carefully checked the progress in my mould and budding crystals.

"Nothing," I told him when I'd recorded everything. "I think this one is another dead end."

"Not everything blooms at the same time."

"I know. It's just that I have some ideas that might have meant I'd make a little extra money this semester, but it doesn't look like that will pan out." We left the lab and headed for the parking lot. "Are you sure I'm this legendary scientist your people think I am? I feel like a hack."

"You're frustrated," Jaden said. He reached out and awkwardly put an arm around me.

"Let's have pizza tonight. Comfort food."

"I want to text EZ. There are things in her book I don't understand."

"I think you've got the basics down."

He smiled shyly at me, but when we walked into the parking lot, he stiffened. "Mitchell, we are watched."

I only saw the frost covered cars and trees moving wildly in the stiff breeze off the ocean. Shadows sprang like dark cats and then retreated in the wind. I closed my eyes, trying to feel something of what was working on Jaden.

"Hey, I caught you!" EZ waved from where she was leaning against my rusty Honda.

"Shit, EZ, you gave me a scare."

Jaden didn't take his gaze off our surroundings.

"Sorry. I wanted to catch you before you left. I spent some time pumping Riley's girlfriend and made up a list of possibles for our bad guy," EZ said. She took a small flash drive out of her bag. "Voilà."

I took it from her. "You're my girl."

"Yep." She looked at Jaden, frowning a little. "You okay?"

He glanced at her. "I am not."

"Oh." She chewed her lip. "Maybe I can help. There's a yoga nidra class in the morning."

"Yoga nidra?" Jaden obviously couldn't help himself.

"Yeah, it's all about tuning into our vibrational self."

I sighed in resignation. "I'll bring him. We better get going. Want me to drop you somewhere?"

"No, I'm good."

I felt uneasiness shift through me at Jaden's continued hyper-alertness. "EZ, we'll walk you to your next class."

"Mitchell!"

"Just let us do it. Jaden thinks someone's watching us."

"Really?" EZ looked intrigued rather than alarmed. "Maybe I can get my own sexy alien."

"You would not like him," Jaden said. "He would not appreciate your vibrational self."

EZ laughed but then sobered after another glance at Jaden. "Hey, you're really worried."

"How could I not worry? You are Mitchell's."

EZ's eyes filled. She scrubbed them briskly. "All right. Damn. I have women's philosophy in A building. That should be enough to kill my tender emotions."

I slung an arm around her and Jaden walked beside us, guarding us. Nothing he'd done had made me like him more than the way he took care of my best friend.

"You know, yoga can be very erotic with a partner," she told me. "It lights up the chakras."

I didn't say anything, but I think my blush gave me away.

"Ohhhh. You two have done it. I knew it!"

"Shut up," I muttered, but of course she steamrolled over me, just like always.

"It was on campus. A broom closet? That's a classic."

"Not a broom closet," Jaden said helpfully. "It was th—" I covered his mouth.

"Hey!" EZ complained. "I was getting my vicarious thrills here."

"You'll have to get them somewhere else." I gave Jaden a death stare. "Discretion."

"We'll carve out a little time at yoga tomorrow," EZ told Jaden. "You can be the nice naïve alien and tell me all about having sex with Mitchell." She was laughing as she headed up the stone steps under the brick archway to her classroom.

My gut clenched, watching her. Love…and fear. "I can't let anything happen to her, ever," I told Jaden. "We have to keep her safe."

"I know." Of course he did, since he'd been watching me. "She's your family."

"That means our enemy might strike at me through her."

Jaden nodded. "He's been watching you as long as I have, Mitchell. He'd see her as a weakness."

It gave me a creepy feeling. "And how would he see what you and I shared in the clock tower?"

"He would see it as me making you my pet," Jaden said. "He would not see how you ensnared me."

"Ensnared you, huh?" I liked that idea. Made me feel more empowered. "I'd like to do it again—after I get some more work done." I'd lost a lot of time on my current experiments because of being so run-down. Now I felt energised. Apparently the strange sex with my alien lover had a side benefit.

I reached for Jaden's hand just as the windows in EZ's class room imploded.

Jaden shoved me to the grass. "Energy blast!"

Heat rolled out in an angry cloud above us, but Jaden protected me with his body.

"Let go!" I pushed him, freeing myself. The air tasted like burnt lint. I ran up the stone steps I'd seen EZ take just minutes ago. I smashed through the door, flying down the hallway. Ash and sparks and smoke were snowing down through silty hot air. I screamed EZ's name, grabbing the doorknob to her classroom. With a hiss, I jerked my hand back.

I tore at my T-shirt, yanking it off to wrap it protectively around my hand.

Jaden hit the door with his shoulder and it crashed open.

Inside it glowed with the embers of hell, crouched students in silhouette, moans.

"EZ!" I yelled. *"Goddamnit, EZ!"*

Jaden grabbed a young woman as she staggered, then pushed her towards the door. She clutched her arm, eyes dazed.

"Have you seen EZ?" I asked two guys further down the stairs. The first one shook his head, then knelt beside his friend, murmuring to him.

I stumbled where the wood had buckled on the steps. Hands reached for me, but they weren't EZ's hands. I tugged another young woman from where she'd been crouched. Her face was smeared with soot, but otherwise she looked okay. "Get out," I croaked, throat caked from the smoke. "Get out now."

I reached podium level. Jaden was helping the professor to her feet, checking her out. My eyes streamed from the heat, but I couldn't find my friend. I couldn't find her.

"Mitch!"

I crushed EZ in my arms, then pulled back to look her over frantically. "You're not hurt!"

"I was in the woman's john." She was trembling. "There's this cute guy in class and I wanted to refresh my lipstick. Stupid and female of me."

"Thank Christ for stupid and female!"

"I heard you screaming my name."

Fire alarms belatedly shrilled and water poured down in wet, charcoal streams. Security arrived while Jaden and I and EZ helped two more young women from the classroom and then the firemen barrelled in, assisting more dazed students outside.

We walked slowly to the Student Union building. EZ slid down to the hallway floor outside the cafeteria, pushing her hair back. "Mom. Oh, shit, I need to call her, but I lost my bag. I think it's back in the bathroom." She got up as if to return, but I grabbed her arm.

"I'll contact her." I did, and then showed EZ the text.

"She's already on her way." EZ's eyes welled again. "I can't believe no one was killed. But what caused that explosion?"

I looked at Jaden. His face had hardened, all prominent narrow bones. "Stay here," he ordered. "Take care of your friend, Mitchell."

"Jaden!" But he was already striding away and I didn't want to leave EZ.

"I was so scared, Mitch," EZ said, leaning against me.

"I know. Me too." I pressed her head against my shoulder. I could have lost her. This whole thing had been so unreal, even thrilling, but what had happened in that classroom had brought it home. People had been hurt and I could have lost my best friend.

"Mitch, that guy is staring at you," EZ whispered.

I tensed, looking down the hallway. There were so many students and faculty milling around I couldn't see whom she meant.

"The redhead. I think he's in Riley's fraternity, but I don't remember his name. He's studying engineering."

I spotted him, let my gaze flick past his grey eyes. "He might be staring at you."

"Yeah, right, like I'd go out with an engineer," EZ sneered.

"They aren't all sexist." But I remembered him dimly. From the Halloween party? When I looked for him again, he'd faded into the crowd.

EZ's mother bolted down the hallway and hugged EZ and then hugged me. She had a lot of power in her hugs, probably all that yoga.

"I'm okay, Mom."

"You need to meditate immediately as a catharsis."

"Mom!"

"After a hot bath. Are you sure you're okay?"

EZ nodded. "Mitchell found me."

"Of course he did." EZ's mom hugged me again and I tried not to wince in an unmanly fashion. "Mitchell, you should come home with us."

Whoa, no way. I'd be in for some kind of aura healing as well as a bubble bath. "I'm waiting for Jaden."

"Jaden's Mitchell's new boyfriend," EZ said.

"I know," EZ's mom said, pushing back her short, salt-and-pepper-blonde hair.

Of course she knew. She'd seen us together at her cafe and had obviously drawn the correct conclusion.

Before EZ could leave with her mom for a hearty vegetarian dinner and a ritual cleansing, I pulled her aside. "Don't go anywhere alone."

"Mitchell!"

"Promise me, EZ. I think there was more to what happened than a damaged vent or whatever." From the mutterings of the students, that was what was going around, that the electrical system had somehow malfunctioned.

She chewed her lip. "All right."

I slouched against the wall after she left, feeling depressed. Should I leave or wait for Jaden? I didn't even have his phone number, if he even had a phone.

I slid down until I was sitting against the wall and put my head on my knees, closing my eyes. Earlier I'd felt great, but now too many thoughts whirled around in my head, colliding like crashed cars. I had to figure out a way to keep EZ safe, to keep her from getting killed by a powerful assassin who could wear any face.

Jaden's hand on my shoulder woke me. "You fell asleep."

I stretched. "I figured I was better off staying here and waiting for you with so many people around."

He nodded, but his face was tight.

"Did you find out what happened?"

"There was an energy signature to the blast," Jaden said. "But to mundane eyes, the explosion seems to have been some foul-up in the heating system."

"Yeah, I'd heard that. That would suit Mr X, since you said he had to be discreet." I took the flash drive EZ had given me out of my pocket. "We have to find out who he is and stop him."

Jaden hesitated.

"What?"

"From the resonance I caught in the classroom debris, he is stronger than I am, ancient and powerful. I am only a young warrior, Mitchell."

I swallowed tightly. "So we'll just have to be smarter."

Chapter Eight

It was when I was locking my front door that it hit me. I turned to glare at Jaden. "It didn't occur to you that it was important to tell me earlier that our enemy might be more formidable than you are?"

"I didn't know." He looked annoyed, not apologetic. Typical alien alpha male. The books I illustrated were plastered with them. Just my bad luck he was the real thing.

"But you suspected..." I rubbed my bottom lip, studying the dishevelled dark beauty of him standing with his hands on his hips, his hair falling out of his makeshift ponytail. His olive skin had the sheen of youth in the starlight, giving him a vulnerability that was not remotely comforting after tonight's attack.

He sighed. "Yes, I suspected I was outmatched. It is why I did not reveal myself to you until your illness forced my hand."

I nodded. "Okay."

"You will have to make do with me as your protector." He was clearly still pissed off.

"Yeah, guess so."

My flippancy obviously grated on him. He tapped one finger on his hip, a nervous tell I remember the real Jaden using sometimes.

"Why did Mr X go after EZ tonight?"

"To draw you into the building. If you'd somehow been killed while trying to rescue her…"

"Bingo, an accident. Poor, heroic, conveniently dead me. But he could have hit the building again. Brought it down with another energy blast."

"Then it would have been clear it wasn't an accident."

"So he'll try again."

"Yes," Jaden said, looking suddenly colourless under the grey light. "I must replenish myself."

"Eat?"

He staggered and I grabbed his arm. "Hey!"

"I must consume material and then rest." His tone made it imperative. I didn't argue with him, since my knowledge of human-alien hybrid health was zilch. And I was also tired and hungry and depressed and pissed off.

We made a gloomy pair as we entered the kitchen.

Jaden sat down at the kitchen table, watching me expectantly.

"What, you think I'm going to cook you dinner?"

"I do not know how to cook," Jaden said stiffly.

"Oh, no. We're not starting this…relationship off on the wrong foot. I barely leave my laboratory when I'm involved with my work, so if you don't cook, you don't eat."

"But you had sex with me," Jaden blurted. He snapped his mouth shut a second later when I seared him with a look. "That is…I have heard commercials on television say the way to a man's heart is through his stomach."

"What makes you think I'm interested in your heart?" I drawled.

He looked uncomfortable. "EZ says you need to be romanced."

"And it's so romantic cooking for a guy in my half-clean kitchen?"

"No. Yes." He shoved his hair out of his eyes. "There is no good answer to that question, Mitchell."

"That's the first smart thing you've said since we got home."

He stared at me and I realised I'd called it home, as in the plural, as in his and my home. Shit. "On your feet, soldier," I growled.

Jaden groaned but did as I ordered. He did still look pale, so his freckles stood out. I decided not to make tonight's lesson too harsh. "You can gather the ingredients for an exotic, fun-filled night of pasta."

"Pasta. I have wanted to eat it. You have it nearly every night, so it must be good," he said wistfully.

"Yeah, except when I'm flush and can order pizza." EZ's mom despaired over my diet. But hey, it was vegetarian. Meat was just too expensive.

"Start with two pans, the really big one in the pull-out drawer first. Fill it up with water and then add some salt and oil."

Jaden had to be directed to where things were and he appeared to have an odd fear of appliances, something about them being very primitive. Despite that, his help meant that we had the pot bubbling in record time. I dropped pasta stuffed with ricotta and spinach into the water, deciding I might as well make a meal he'd really enjoy, since it was his first time having my favourite staple.

"Can we try Indian food sometime?" he asked as he watched me stir the pot.

I smiled at him, my depression lifting. He was like a kid sometimes with his desire to explore our world, so I couldn't stay mad at him. "Yeah. There's a good local place with great curry."

"I want to try the chickpea curry."

I had that often, since it was the cheapest on the menu. "Tomorrow night, if Mr X doesn't put in another appearance."

He nodded gravely. "EZ is coming over in the morning to go over the contents of the flash drive with us. Perhaps we will find a clue."

"You're not just a fantasy, are you?" I watched our dinner cook, stirring occasionally. I couldn't look at him, thinking even an innocent alien would be able to read between those lines.

"You wanted me to be like the sexy alien with the purple eyes?" he asked me, referring to my latest romance illustration. "All powerful. Not someone who could be hurt."

I rubbed the back of my neck. "Yeah, I guess I got caught up in the fantasy when I met you."

"I did try to find an attractive human male with purple eyes, Mitchell," he admitted earnestly.

Aw. How could I not melt? My alien lover had searched for a body with eyes he thought I'd like. "I love your eyes..."

"I would die the true death to protect you, but even that might not be enough."

I put down the spoon. "Wait, what's the 'true' death?" I didn't like the sound of that.

"My people are immortal unless our energy is intentionally dissipated by another. That is the true death."

I swallowed, picturing his soul shredded like mist in sunlight. "Mr X can do that to you?"

"Yes."

"I won't let him."

"Mitchell," he sighed.

"I won't."

"Remarkably unscientific for you to say that."

The pasta was ready so I poured out the hot water and began to mix the sauce. Jaden watched avidly. He was still pale and I didn't like that. We'd have to experiment to see what his limits were in Jaden's body.

"Sit down. Eat."

He sat, and when I served him dinner, he ate without further conversation, completely focused on refuelling. I poured him two glasses of milk and found some two-day-old doughnuts in the pantry. He ate them and then half a bag of carrots.

"Okay now?"

"The pasta was good." He looked at my half-finished plate. I slid it to him and put my chin in my hand as he devoured my leftovers. Watching him eat like that sent a curl of heat through my backbone. He'd been like that making love, totally focused.

He looked up at me through his lashes. "Very good," he murmured around a mouth full of food.

Now I sighed. "I'll see if there's more."

He gave one of his slightly off-kilter smiles.

"I want to work in your laboratory tomorrow," he announced after he'd finished all the pasta.

I bristled but then took a deep breath. "I don't like sharing my space. I have to do it at school but here at home…"

"I won't touch your works in progress," he said. "But I need time alone to create a detection device to help locate our adversary."

"Yeah?" Now that I could get behind. Besides, it would be fascinating to see him build it. "I want to help."

He nodded. "It will be an energy construct. You should appreciate it since you have an intuitive mind with science."

"Science saved me. If I didn't have it, I don't know what I would have done."

"I watched you when you were a child. You were neglected by your aunt and uncle. You spent a lot of time alone then too."

I swallowed. "It was okay. It just helped me hone my discipline."

"You should have been loved for the special person you are." When I raised a brow at the unaccustomed sentimentality from him, he added, "No, you are correct—I do not fully understand the concept of love, but I have seen children who are valued. The people who raised you were not worthy."

"EZ would say that my past was the manure that made the rose grow."

Jaden's expression didn't quite lighten. "She would. She is exceptional."

"You look better. Not so pale."

"I must rest and restore for a time. Your sleeping shelf will prove adequate."

"Dandy."

"Ah… Will you share it with me, Mitchell? I like the custom of your people."

"What custom is that?"

"Sleeping together."

I took his hand as he tugged me insistently from the kitchen. I'd been tired and depressed and bruised. Suddenly I was plastered against the wall, his heart slamming against mine, his lips covering mine in a clumsy, ardent kiss.

"No," I whispered. "Let me show you." I wasn't any hot shot in the kissing department, since there had only been Riley before Jaden, but in my fantasies I'd lived out kissing a thousand men, tasting them, nipping their lips, running my tongue along skin. With Jaden, as soon as our lips met there had been a crackle in the air, as if from a kind of manic electricity. Blue sparks went off around us like firecrackers. He moaned, gripping my hips.

"Wait…"

"Mitchell."

"Trust me."

He laid his head against my shoulder in surrender, his chest rising and falling fast. "Yes."

"Look at me, baby," I said. When he raised his head I saw his irises had been devoured by the black of his pupils. Colour flagged his cheeks. Apparently my pasta had recharged him with a vengeance. "Let me kiss you."

He shuddered as I used the tip of my tongue to tease him, outlining his full pouty bottom lip. He definitely had been gifted with the face of a poet, more Lord Byron now than Mr Darcy.

He gasped as I penetrated him with my tongue, taking him so he groaned again, shivering wildly from just this tiny touch.

Power pulsed in the air around us, the sparks glittering in jewel tones of ruby, sapphire and amethyst, and that power was also inside me, for the first time in my life, hot and soaring, like I was a bird flying over a forest fire.

As I tutored him in kissing me, I couldn't help but reach out and cup him where he was as ready as I was, as stiff and aching.

He pressed himself eagerly into my hand, his eyes heavy lidded as I stroked him.

"Good boy," I said.

He growled. Apparently my big, bad alien didn't like being called a boy. It made me grin.

"Mitchell." His tone was a warning.

I hooked a leg around him and he leaned against me, his body quivering. Just like that, I won. He would let me take control.

He was mine.

The heat melted into something soft and fuzzy. Oh shit. I didn't want to put a name to it.

My moment of weakness was too much of a delay for Jaden. He raised my arms above my head. Then he took over the kissing lessons, bumping noses with me once, but then… Oh, yeah, he licked me like I was his favourite ice cream.

I wrapped myself around him, so desperate from just our kissing game. His hand tangled in my hair, dislodging my glasses so they fell to the floor beside us. "You don't need those."

"Yeah, I do."

"No. Close your eyes, Mitchell."

"What are you up to?" I asked him suspiciously.

"Shhhh."

He'd trusted me and now he was asking that I trust him. "Okay." I closed my eyes and felt the warmth of his body close to mine, felt the pulsing of my excitement and the tingling of my lips from kissing him. Jaden gently brushed my eyelids and I felt lightning zap through my skull.

I snapped my eyes open, vision swirling. And then his face sharpened, came into focus.

"Holy shit…" I breathed. I could see him perfectly, even better than with my scratched glasses.

"I can take away all your hurts," he said. "I can take away that neglect in your childhood; erase it from your memory."

"Whoa," I panted. I couldn't think about the implications of his offer right now. I grabbed his head and kissed him and we fought to get closer, clunking against the stairs, his hand rubbing me through my pants.

The sparks danced around us like we were creating our own personal bonfire. But I didn't care about his unique abilities right now. I didn't care about anything but his body against mine, his harsh breathing and the sweat that gleamed on his forehead.

We couldn't break apart long enough to strip. I could barely grab air for my lungs.

"I need you." I'd never said it to another person. His hair was tangled in my hand, his neck under my lips, his body working against mine…

"Mitchell!" His back arched as he thrust against me.

"Jesus!"

I came, pressed against him so I felt the answering quiver of his release.

We held on to each other. If we'd let go, I think we both would have fallen. The sparks around us gentled to soft fireflies, revolving lazily around our bodies as we slumped, gasping, onto the stairs.

"Jaden," I said, clearing my throat because my voice sounded so hoarse.

"Y-yes?" He gave me a look of concern. "You are all right, Mitchell?"

"Peachy." I couldn't stop from combing fingers through that tumbled dark hair. "I don't want to forget. I appreciate the eye renovation but..." I chewed my lip. "I'm the man I am, the scientist I am, because of my past."

He turned his head into my caress, obviously enjoying being petted. "You taught me to kiss," he said simply. "I like you."

I grinned. "You know, so do I." I hadn't for a while, letting the incident with Riley make me feel shitty. Hell with that.

Chapter Nine

EZ, Jaden and I all sat on pillows on the floor in my laboratory the next morning.

"All we need is a sitar to complete this picture," EZ joked. "I feel like George Harrison."

"If I have to move, I don't want to bother with much stuff," I reminded her. What furniture there was in my laboratory were long tables holding equipment I'd borrowed, bought or modified on my own.

When I'd woken that morning, Jaden had been gone from the single bed we'd shared. I'd found him standing in the middle of my lab, his eyes closed, his arms outstretched, his brow furrowed. Creating the special energy construct he'd mentioned the night before?

I'd brought him a bowl of cereal and then worked on one of my projects until EZ arrived.

"Here's some lattes so we don't go completely sixties," she said, passing me and then Jaden a steaming paper cup.

Jaden sniffed it where the steam rose from the little opening. "Coffee. This was one of the things I was most curious to try." He took a gulp and then closed his eyes.

EZ gave me an amused look. "I guess he likes it."

"Not as much as orgasms," he mumbled around his drink. "Mitchell gives me many."

"Oh, do tell," EZ drawled.

I flushed, which only seemed to amuse her more. "Um. Okay, on to our suspect list."

EZ sobered and then pulled out a spreadsheet from her messenger bag. "I made a shortlist last night. I'm assuming whoever's body Mr X, uh, took over, would be someone who had relatively close contact with Mitch on Halloween so he or she could pass on the virus."

Jaden nodded, pausing to inhale more coffee aroma as if it were perfume.

"And you don't think Mr X was that scum Riley?" she asked him.

"No. When a body has been used by one of my kind, there is a…residue of energy," Jaden said. "I have not seen traces in Riley. But he is scum. He is garbage to be walked on."

EZ laughed and I flushed again. "Jaden, Jeez!"

He narrowed his eyes at me. "I do not like how that human treated you. He trifled with your feelings in some kind of…game."

I sighed because I could see another sign of Jaden's innocence. He just couldn't get why Riley would pull that kind of trick. Well, I couldn't explain it to him since I didn't know either. That kind of thinking…it just eluded me.

"It didn't make him happy," I said. "And now he'll never have me."

"His loss," Jaden growled.

I laughed. "Thanks. Now back to our suspect list."

"Two people I think we should check out first," EZ said. "Riley's girlfriend..."

"—But Jaden said he could pick up residue if someone had been taken over..." I began.

"Wait." EZ held up her hand. "He may not have used her directly on Halloween night, but she's tight with Riley and his crowd. At the very least we should question her. She'd know if anyone close to Riley has been behaving oddly."

"Okay." Good point. I had forgotten how smart EZ was about people, probably from running the yoga studio and vegetarian cafeteria with her mother for so many years. I tended to prefer to hide from people, so I hadn't developed her edge.

"Our second and far more viable suspect is that creepy redheaded engineering student Mitch and I spotted after the explosion on campus. I did some research. His name is Mason Anderson and he attended the Halloween party."

"So we hunt them down on campus and..." I blinked. Looked at Jaden. "You said you could build some kind of device to detect our opponent?"

Jaden nodded, then closed his eyes and sucked in a deep breath. Of course, the strain on his face only made him look hotter, muscles bulging, dark hair tangled over his brow. He probably looked great working out in a gym, while I usually looked like I was fighting constipation. "I will ensure that you and EZ will recognise our enemy."

"How?" EZ looked intrigued.

For an answer, Jaden raised his palm and energy shot from it, surrounding her in an orange swirling ball.

She gasped, her body jerking as she writhed inside the energy sphere. Her body lit up, not merely her physical body, but the air around it in several bright, rainbow shades. For a moment she resembled a lion fish, spikes of colour bristling around her, and I realised I was actually seeing her aura. Then the light show snuffed out and she wavered on her feet.

"Jesus!" I roared, going to her and crushing her limp body close. "What did you do?" I glared accusingly at Jaden.

He was pale and sweating, but his eyes gleamed with a kind of eerie heat. "I lent her a part of myself. She will now be able to feel Mr X if he is in close proximity. She will also have other…abilities, although I'm not sure how they will manifest."

"Abilities?" EZ wheezed, a hand pressed over her heart chakra. "Will I be able to do hot yoga?"

Jaden looked confused. "I don't know."

"Sorry, bad joke. I feel different…" She bit her lip. "Not bad different, Mitch, so don't get all protective."

"You could have warned her!" I was still glaring at Jaden, who looked clueless.

Jaden blinked. "Why?"

"Mitch, we can't argue about this now," EZ interrupted. "We have to find the bad guy. Besides, look at him…" EZ gave Jaden a worried look. "You don't look so good, honey."

"I am…fine," Jaden whispered.

"Hey." I touched his forehead. "You're like ice!"

His lips curved in his awkward smile. "I am almost at the limits of what I can share with you and EZ. Much more and I will be trapped in this frail human form." He lifted a wrist to illustrate.

"You mean you'd have to stay Jaden forever?" I could feel one of those tension headaches brewing. The kind I got when I was trying to grasp a particularly difficult problem.

Jaden held my gaze. "Yes. I'd need this body to continue. I only have enough reserves to fight with my enemy now, after… It doesn't matter."

"It does matter," I muttered.

"Wait!" EZ waved a hand. "I'm having an epiphany!"

"You look like you're giving birth."

"What's with your fascination with me having a kid?" She poked me. "Probably a latent desire to have kids. Fair enough. I wouldn't mind being inseminated with your super-smart sperm one day. We could share the child."

"What? Uh." EZ did that, jumped from A to Z; it was the root of her nickname. I wasn't going to touch the bizarre baby-plan idea. "What's your epiphany?"

"If Jaden can be reduced by expending energy, why can't we do that to Mr X?" She whirled to look at Jaden, who was still pale, hair matted to his damp brow. "Our opponent's probably still winded from that big energy ball he whizzed at the classroom. If we find him and can make him spend more energy…"

"We can weaken him," Jaden finished. "Take away his ability to do harm. Yes, it might work."

"He wouldn't just...stay stuck in a human body, would he?" I asked Jaden. "You said he was a fanatic about how superior your people are in their natural state, so if he loses a round with us, if we manage to best him—"

"He will choose non-existence over being trapped in inferior flesh," Jaden agreed. He closed his eyes. "I need…a moment."

"Jaden, you're not feeding me any more of your energy," I told him, letting him lean on me. "Shit, you're limp as a sleepy puppy."

He was breathing deeply. "I am never limp around you, Mitchell."

EZ giggled.

"Ah, right. Good to know." I couldn't resist pushing the hair off his sweaty forehead. He was both chilly and perspiring, like he had a weird tropical fever. "I can't take anything from you. Not when it leaves you wasted like this."

His eyes opened and he looked into me. "It doesn't matter. All that matters is you."

My throat got that stupid burn. I swallowed around it. "Don't start with that protector business or you'll piss me off. EZ and I are going to do our share, help even the odds, but you are not sacrificing yourself for me."

He only shook his head. Stubborn, gorgeous alien.

"Are you going to be up to hunting with us on campus?"

"I will eat again and restore myself," he said.

"Maybe there's another solution." I rubbed my upper lip, considering. "When we, uh, exchange matrix patterns, I feel energised. Does it work both ways?"

Jaden's eyes widened. "Yes. But—"

I stroked his chest. "You're no good to me worn out. Let's try an experiment." I wished I had time to rig something up to measure our exchange, but we were most likely to run our quarry down if we headed to campus in time for morning classes.

"An experiment," he repeated. He took my hand almost hesitantly and placed it under his T-shirt so it was resting on his bare chest.

My breathing picked up as I stared into his eyes. I was aware of his heart thudding.

"Nothing's happening," I finally said.

He swallowed. "I have not recovered. It is hard to bring up an energy flare."

"Maybe it just needs a spark." Forgetting all about EZ, who I figured was watching us avidly, I leant forward and brushed my lips against his.

Fire ignited as my tongue touched his. I experienced it on a physical level, that delicious feel of his hard body wrapping possessively around mine, his silky hair in my fist, his heart thundering under my burning palm. I felt it on an energy level, sensed the glow of light through my closed eyelids, felt him come inside me in a way that was more intimate than sex.

At first it was like hot fingers exploring me, my thoughts and emotions, but then Jaden's essence caged me and he dived into the darker parts, where Riley had touched me. Jaden tackled those memories with the psychic equivalent of scrubbing bubbles.

"Stop!" I ordered him mentally. We were so close I knew he could read my thoughts.

"He will not have you. Not any part of you."

Jealousy. My alien boyfriend was jealous as hell. I felt the flames of it sear me as he shot light into the memories of Riley touching me, then betraying me. Jaden had no conception of how trivial my fling with Riley was. To him, I had to be his, all his, my body, my emotions.

"Don't. He doesn't matter anymore," I whispered to him. I could feel Jaden's torment. He was living my past pain as if it were his own.

"He hurt you. I feel it."

Jaden knew how I'd felt on top of the world as Riley kissed me, put his mouth on my cock, made me feel like a lover for the first time in my life. How stupidly naïve I'd been to attend that party with him afterward, thinking he was proud to be with me.

I deliberately yanked Jaden away from those dark splotches of pain that were paling even now under the bleach treatment he was giving my matrix. Instead, I relived our first kiss, the way Jaden's eyes had looked in sunlight, with bits of amber lighting the brown, the way I'd trusted him enough with that terrible vulnerability, letting him inside my body.

"Mitchell..." He drowned himself in me, lighting sparks all through my body and soul so my fingers and toes tingled. His kiss was ravenous, hungry for my taste. He reached down and cupped me, and potency rolled through me. I was hard as iron under his touch, aching, marked by more than just his flesh.

He moaned and I was suddenly underneath him, his body crushing mine, his lips taking me savagely. I twisted his hair to bring him closer, wanting to meld our bodies as closely as our souls.

A gasp broke the moment.

EZ.

Still here and watching us.

I closed my eyes. I would not die of sexual denial.

Jaden squeezed me gently and I nearly came. Damn. He was shameless, but then he didn't have the kind of inhibitions I was saddled with.

Lucky Jaden.

I cleared my throat. "EZ," I rasped. "I guess I can't bribe you to leave the room."

"I'm sorry, Mitch but... We have a mission, remember?"

Shit. I forced myself to clear my throat, to shove Jaden's hand aside. He gave me a hurt look. "You got the zap you needed?" I asked him.

"Zap?" His dark brows furrowed, then his expression cleared. "Yes."

I peeled myself away from him, walking over to the nearest table and gripping it until my body calmed a little. I was definitely energised. I didn't want to analyse the emotional hangover from being so close to Jaden. It actually hurt not to be a part of him.

EZ wasn't looking at me with the taunting smile I'd expected. She actually looked a little embarrassed. "Sorry. But this is too important to—"

"No problem." I cleared my throat again because my voice was still dark and husky with arousal. "Thanks."

"Sure."

"You will not take more energy from me?" Jaden asked.

I shook my head. "We'll split up and see if we can find Mason or Mallory. I'll just have to use my old-fashioned human senses to figure out if one of them is acting strange."

"I can stick with Mitchell, Jaden," EZ offered. "I feel…fantastic."

"Very well. I will try to trace the energy signature I scented last night," Jaden said. "It might be another path to finding our enemy." He stood and a look of pain flickered over his face.

"What?" I demanded, immediately concerned.

"I am…frustrated. It is painful." He glared at me.

"Join the club," I said.

"Guys, can we focus? Not that the merging wasn't…" She licked her lips. "It was beautiful, the glowing light surrounding you, the way you kissed."

This was extremely sentimental coming from my EZ. I avoided her eyes. "Okay, Jaden, you should—"

He was already gone. I ran a hand through my hair. "Well, that was an abrupt exit."

"I think we need to train him to say goodbye," EZ said.

"Mmmm."

We took a little longer, getting rid of the coffee paraphernalia and me grabbing a heavy coat. "Let's go hunting, my girl," I said.

But EZ stopped me after I'd locked my door. "Mitch, you're in love with Jaden, aren't you?"

Chapter Ten

"What did you say?"

"I think I was clear enough." EZ glared at me. "You are so in love with Jaden. What are you going to do about it?"

I gulped in a deep breath but unfortunately I didn't safely beam to an alternative universe where EZ wasn't grilling me about my romantic life. "What can I do?" I hedged.

"Ah-ha! A tacit admission of love. So guy-like."

"I *am* a guy."

"Exactly. And you're in love with Jaden."

"Can we please focus on the mission?" I was willing to beg. This topic was like a sharp stick poking into my gut.

"How are you going to keep him with us—keep Jaden, I mean," EZ continued, with all the ruthlessness of a very good friend. Damn, she always thought she knew what was best for me. Trouble was, she usually did.

"I'm supposed to keep him?" I doled out an extra helping of sarcasm but it didn't seem to faze her.

"Well, yeah. He can be the model for all your future romance covers."

"Yeah, he—" I blinked. "Hey, you tried to trick me!"

"Duh. Don't tell me you can't picture your cute alien boyfriend living with you."

I could, but I didn't see how it would work out. "We're literally from two different worlds."

"So are men and women."

"Yeah, yeah, don't start on that men are from Mars crap."

"It should be easier for you to understand and live with a man because you have a dick," she said. "And all that crazy-making testosterone."

"A match made in heaven."

"Mitchell." She grabbed my arm. "He came through time and space for *you.* Are you going to let him turn into a big vapour cloud when this is all over and walk out of your life?"

"I don't think vapour clouds walk."

She narrowed her eyes.

"I'm crazy about him." My voice cracked. I looked away immediately. "Stop. We are not having this conversation."

"Fine. I gave you something to think about. Use all those super smarts and come up with a way you can keep your star-crossed honey."

I stared up at a black nightmare of twisted metal, at the jagged spikes of a broken windshield that spilled glass like diamonds on the black velvet pedestal.

"It's eerie," EZ said in a hushed voice as we walked through the exhibit featuring crashed cars and bikes in the fine arts wing on campus. "This motorcycle fortunately was not involved in a fatal accident like some of the others. I never took our girl Mallory for being such a morbid budding artist."

"Guess dating Riley has this effect on her."

"Yeah, twisting her like all of these wrecks." EZ grimaced but then frowned. "You know what these also bring to mind? Jaden. Makes me think of him and his motorcycle crash. I know he had no family, the real Jaden, I mean. He was a foster kid and a loner. All he ever seemed to have was that bike of his."

"He didn't have anyone," I agreed.

"No, but now he has us."

"EZ!" Mallory smiled her cheerleader smile, white teeth gleaming. Looking at her I remembered how stupid I'd felt, thinking Riley would take me over her. "Oh and…ah, your friend."

"You know very well this is Mitchell, Mal," EZ said. Her tone was all *'don't bullshit me, you know he slept with your boyfriend'*.

Mallory gave me a vicious look. Apparently I was more of a threat than I'd thought. I should probably be flattered. "I know who he is. Riley's pathetic little experiment."

I laughed. "Well, I am a scientist."

"What do you want? He's over that phase, if you think you'll hop in bed with the two of us."

"What?" I laughed again. "No… I guess you could say I'm over my Riley phase."

She didn't look like she believed me.

EZ rolled her eyes. "Mitch has more pride than to sleep with you in order to get close to Riley."

"For the record, I couldn't sleep with Mallory. I could sleep with you, EZ, if I had to, but Mallory isn't a nice person." I took my glasses off and cleaned them on my T-shirt.

EZ sighed. "Can I pick a great best friend? He'd even sacrifice himself to sleep with me."

I laughed but obviously Mallory didn't see the humour.

"What do you two want?" Mallory growled. She was trembling. Abruptly, I felt sorry for her. She was building her dream life with Riley out of mud bricks. First good rain would bring it down.

"We want to know if you've noticed anyone in your crowd acting strange lately," EZ said. She had as much subtlety as the business end of a bat.

"You mean other than you two?"

"It's important, Mallory," EZ pressed.

"Well, Jaden's certainly lost his mind. Word is he hit his gorgeous head in his motorcycle crash, because why else would he be dating Mitchell?"

"Please," I muttered, not impressed by her show of cattiness.

"It was a pretty bad accident," Mallory said, looking a little deflated that I wasn't hurt. "That's his former bike. I got it from the junk yard." She nodded towards the black Harley EZ and I had been staring at when she'd joined us. My belly twisted, imagining Jaden's blood spattered on it.

But Jaden was alive. He had walked away from that accident and blasted through my front door and into my life.

A miracle.

My throat had that irritating burn again. I swallowed around it. "Look, I didn't know you and Riley were still hooked up on Halloween. It may not matter to you, but no matter how beautiful he is, I wouldn't have gone out with him if I'd known he had someone."

Mallory blinked. "You are a naïve child."

"Yeah, I was."

She chewed her lip, considering me, then blew out a breath. "All right, I believe you and... Yeah, one of Riley's friends has been behaving...differently. You could say he's why I'm hiding out here today." Colour washed through her pale cheeks.

"Is it Mason?" EZ demanded.

"Yes," Mallory said, sounding surprised that we'd guessed. Her gaze fell for the first time. "Now leave me the hell alone, both of you."

I took EZ's arm before she could say more. We were silent walking through the gauntlet of all those shattered cars and bikes, shattered dreams.

Mallory's artistic world was as depressing as her real one.

"It was a bit off the wall, prodding me about a threesome," I said. "I thought it was a joke."

"She's desperate." EZ and I stepped into the elevator that would take us back to the main level. "And I bet she's had a threesome before for old Riley's benefit."

"Maybe...with Mason?"

EZ blinked. "Oh, shit. You think Mr X was curious about what it was like to couple with humans?"

"If Mason is our man, he used Riley and Mallory as an experiment while he was waiting to pop me."

EZ shuddered. "It wouldn't have been anything like you and Jaden."

"No. Jaden would never use someone like that, even if he is curious."

"He's in love with you too, you know," EZ said.

"EZ, he doesn't even know what love is." I stuffed my hands in my pockets. "I'm not sure I do."

"Oh yeah he does. Because we just saw its opposite with Mallory and, like you said, Jaden would never do that, use you as a cold experiment in human-alien relations."

No, there was nothing cold when Jaden touched me. He always acted like he couldn't keep his hands off me and God knows I felt the same.

"What next, we hunt down Mason?"

"I think we should head to the cafe in the SUB building and try to meet up with Jaden, get his take on what Mallory told us," she said, referring to the most popular coffee shop on campus. "Everyone goes through there at least once a day so we might spot him. The one thing I think we should avoid right now is contact with Mason until we have some serious backup."

I nodded. "Our opponent is ruthless."

"Yes. I know Mr X firebombed a classroom, but I didn't get how ruthless until we talked to Mallory." She made a face. "Maybe it's a girl thing, but the idea of being so coldly used for sex…"

"It's not a girl thing. I'm a scientist and I find it repugnant."

"You're an ethical scientist," EZ said. "You have a genuine desire to make people's lives better with your inventions."

I coloured but fortunately she didn't continue. We found a table near the smoky glass windows overlooking the concrete courtyard, where we could see students pass by on the way to class. "Maybe Jaden's love of coffee will make him show up soon," EZ said. "I have a theory about the coffee love—it probably lights up his energy matrix."

"That's interesting." I was itching to do some experiments with Jaden, to see what could enhance his powers. Too bad we were being hunted so I didn't have time. "But whatever happens, remember our opponent is after *me,* EZ," I told her. "Not you."

Her gaze drilled into mine. "I am not going to desert you so that…that thing can just kill you."

"He nearly killed you before." I took her hand and squeezed it firmly. "It would have killed me."

"Mitchell—"

"No, EZ. I'm scared and I want to put my head in the sand and just…hide. But knowing you could be hurt if I don't handle this, take him out somehow—"

"You don't get to be a hero, pal," she said. "We're a team, you, me and Jaden."

I wanted to take her name from that list but I knew she wouldn't let me.

Friendship was hell on a guy sometimes.

"Don't get sexist and protective."

"I'll cop to protective." A flash of red hair caught my eye, since the grey day outdoors made Mason's hair stand out. "Shit, Mason's coming."

EZ tensed beside me.

I studied the engineering student, seeing that, unlike the other people rushing for class, he wasn't wearing a knapsack heavy with books or carrying a phone or tablet and messaging someone. Instead, his eyes shifted right to left and his walk seemed almost military stiff. His face was expressionless.

"He's creepy. How could Riley have wanted to sleep with him?"

"Riley will sleep with anything with a dick." Not exactly flattering to me, but true.

Mason's gaze suddenly riveted to us as we watched him from our window side table. He shouldn't have been able to see us through the opaque glass but I saw his eyes widen, the colour seeming to intensify and glow.

"EZ..."

"I feel him," she whispered. "Like Jaden, but not. Cold. Like a machine."

Mason was suddenly running towards us.

"He's made us. Up!" I yanked EZ from her chair, upending our lattes and causing the couple next to us to swear. I didn't stop to fumble through an apology but kept hold of EZ and ran.

EZ didn't argue. I heard her panting beside me as we made it to the entrance into the SUB mall. Behind us came the sound of shattering glass. Mason had jumped right through the window to follow us.

"Playtime is over," I huffed. I scanned the crowded hallway and ran towards a door near the entrance, EZ clinging to my hand.

"He's coming, Mitch!"

"I know." I hit the side door and we ran up two flights of stairs.

"Where are we going?" EZ asked.

"Science fiction club meets here every Thursday," I told her, taking out my keys. "I have access to our meeting room."

Behind us, we heard the door to the stairs slam open.

"Oh, Goddess, it's just like a horror movie," EZ said.

"Shhh!"

The steps behind us were even and unhurried, as if Mason knew finding us was a foregone conclusion.

We sprinted as quietly as possible to the door of the science fiction club. I fumbled with the key and then unlocked it, trying to ignore the footsteps getting closer.

I left the light off, dragging EZ deeper into the room with its second-hand furniture and lurid posters of robots carrying away human women. "I never thought

I'd be grateful you're such a nerd," she breathed. "But I don't think we've lost him."

I caught the sound of footsteps now in the hallway behind us.

"Hurry!" EZ and I ran to the door concealed behind a poster of *The X Files*. I wrenched it open.

"A hidden staircase," EZ huffed. "You know all the odd nooks and crannies on campus."

Behind us the door into the club room rattled.

EZ and I ran full out up the hidden stairs, reaching the rusty fire door at the top. I tried my key but it was stubborn, so I tried it again and again, jiggling the door as quietly as possible while sweat broke out on my back.

"We're trapped!" EZ was staring down into the darkness below. "Did you hear something?"

I tried the lock again, closing my eyes and trying to visualise the negative space, the places where metal grated against metal.

After an age, the door swung open and we were on the roof of the SUB building with a killer view of campus, the surrounding woods and the ocean beyond.

"Oh…" EZ wrapped her arms around herself. "Cold and misty up here."

"There's an entrance back into the main mall there." I pointed towards a door about a hundred yards away. We crunched gravel underfoot as we ran for it. "Keep moving."

The door slammed open behind us.

"Mitchell!" EZ screamed.

Mason stood behind us, eyes fixed on me.

"EZ, run!"

But I should have remembered how she always thought she knew what was best for me.

Mason raised his hand, palm up, fingers glowing.

"*No!*" EZ's body flew, coming between me and a red-orange blast of energy from Mason's hand. She grabbed her side, falling to her knees.

"EZ, oh, God!" I grabbed her. She was limp in my arms. She wasn't breathing. She wasn't goddamned breathing.

Pebbles crunched. I looked up into Mason's serene eyes. "You son of a bitch!"

"You must not be allowed to exist," he said. "You are inferior. A mistake. I will erase you."

He raised his hand again.

I scooped up gravel and shot it at his face.

He cried out in pain, holding one eye.

I launched myself at him. Mason played rugby. I was outclassed, but my body, my rage didn't seem to know. I hit him, pounding my fist into his gut over and over again. "You hurt her! You fucking hurt her!"

Mason smiled, holding me off easily. His cool expression was unmoved by my passion. "Inferior."

"Fuck. You."

"You should never have been allowed to live beyond the cradle," Mason said. "My people debated while you grew up, began your experiments. Unacceptable."

"Yeah, having to talk about things in a democracy is a drag." I didn't know if Jaden's people followed a system like ours but I needed his attention on me, not EZ.

"You know nothing of us. Even that traitor would not lower himself to share with you."

"Ha."

Mason frowned, looking back over his shoulder and I had my one shot. I caught the startled look in his eyes as I shoved him off the fucking roof.

Chapter Eleven

I watched Mason fall, his mouth a long, empty shape, elongated horribly to reveal sharpened teeth. In slow motion his body somersaulted over and over, the fall taking forever, as if he was dropping into an endless vortex and not off the SUB building roof.

Even as I watched, helpless, staring into his bulging eyes, they lit, going an uncanny green. Energy shot out from his fingertips and struck my chest, ate into my skin, melting it like pink lace, dissolving bone until acid touched my beating heart –

"Mitchell!"

Jaden's arms locked around me. I buried my face against his neck, sucking in breath. "You're home, you're safe," he said, as he had many, many times over the past five nights.

I clung to him, listening to the steady drum of his heart as the sweat dried on my back. "He wasn't there when I looked over the roof, Jaden. He wasn't fucking there! Just…gone."

"I know. But you hurt him. I could see that in the residue of energy."

After I'd shoved Mason from the roof, Jaden had exploded out of the door EZ and I had used during our escape, speeding to my side, his body a blur it had moved so fast.

"A few crushed shrubs but no sign of him."

"He will need time to recover," Jaden repeated.

"I almost killed a fellow student. I didn't think about that. I just shoved him off the roof."

"There is likely not to be much of Mason left," Jaden said wearily. "Only the most stubborn personality would survive."

I pulled back, wiping my damp palms on my thighs. "What do you mean?"

Jaden shrugged. "Our opponent has been inside him for months, Mitchell. *Months.* It is unlikely there is anything left of Mason."

I swallowed. "Another reason you chose someone who was dying."

Jaden nodded. "Jaden's essence was already gone. I have some of his memories, but it's like an empty house with a few pieces of furniture."

"Right." I sat up, pulling my knees to my chest. "I just wish I'd killed that son of a bitch."

"You damaged him."

"I couldn't stop him from hurting EZ. I couldn't."

"Mitchell…"

"I need to see her." I flung the covers off, knowing without seeing a mirror that I looked like hell. I had barely eaten and slept only in snatches. My time was consumed by the long vigil I lived in my lab.

Jaden followed me up the stairs. I knew he would.

I pushed open the door of my laboratory and squinted at the bright luminescence of the sphere lying on the largest table in the room.

"She looks like Sleeping Beauty. EZ would…" I cleared my throat as I walked closer to the capsule where my best friend slept, her hair tangled around her pale face, swirling mists covering her naked body. "EZ would love that idea. She'd love it even more if we could find a straight prince to kiss her awake. Is she…healing?"

Jaden shook his head. "She would have died outright if she'd not had a part of me in her. I don't know, Mitchell. She sleeps."

I rubbed my gritty eyes. "Yeah. Okay. It's just getting hard to tell her mom she went on a yoga holiday to Costa Rica, you know? Where she isn't allowed to use her phone."

I looked dully at the pile of brochures I'd collected in order to brief EZ on her cover story if—*when* she woke up.

"Mitchell." Jaden's voice was hoarse. "I do not like watching you hurt."

"It's what you do when you're human. Still want to be one of us?"

Jaden didn't say anything, his gaze watchful. Hell, he was handling this so much better than I was, constantly nagging me to eat, standing over me every time I attempted sleep, taking me to class when I absolutely had to go and always, always guarding me.

And I couldn't even reach out and touch him. I didn't care if Jaden watched television or sat next to me while I slept. I stared through him.

I pushed my shaking hands through my greasy hair. Jeez, when was the last time I'd taken a shower or shaved? I could smell myself and I was ripe.

As if he'd read my thoughts, Jaden reached out and tugged me gently to him. "She sleeps and we can do no more for her."

I leaned against him, feeling shaky. My body wanted to cry but I was too worn out.

"Come on," Jaden said. He coaxed me into the bathroom and gently stripped off my clothes as I stood there, holding the towel rack so I didn't fall over.

I heard him switch on the spray and then adjust it. It took him a moment since my old bathroom had a cranky water heater. Then he carefully led me to the tub and under the spray.

He got in with me, fully clothed.

"Hey!"

He looked down at his soaking sweatshirt and jeans and shrugged. "I am warm. I am with you."

I melted. It was that innocence again.

"I'm sorry." I put my arms around him and colour touched his cheekbones that wasn't brought on by the heat of the shower. His eyelids fell.

It was my effect on him. Just being close to me turned him on, made him tremble under my hands. I ran them over his shoulders, down his arms until our fingers meshed. He leaned his forehead against mine and we stood there, shaky legged under the shower.

He cleared his throat. "You need to be cared for."

"So do you."

"I am a tough alien."

I laughed. "Yeah."

"A real son of a bitchin' alien."

"You've been watching Charlie Bronson movies again," I said.

"I need attitude to be a successful human."

"Sure." I kissed him and he gasped as I stroked my tongue over his. He was excited, almost ready to burst. "Soap. You should wash my back," I instructed, deliberately turning away from him. I wanted him so much…but I couldn't let go.

I braced myself against the wet tile. I was shaking like a single leaf left on a tree.

Hesitantly, he picked up a bar of ivory and ran it down my spine to my backbone. I shuddered under the caress, my cock stiff and aching from the light touches. Grimly, I endured it, as I'd endured his closeness, his yearning.

All week he'd even been offering himself to me in his innocent way. I wasn't much more experienced than he was, but even I couldn't miss it.

"Mitchell…" His breath was hot against my neck and his hand shook as he continued to wash me.

I squeezed my eyes shut. "I'm sorry. You deserve so much better than me."

"I won't let you lose her," he promised. "When I no longer need to be strong, I will give her back her vitality."

I snapped around to look at him. "What will that do to *you?*" He didn't answer. "EZ wouldn't want her life back at the cost of yours."

"I was too slow in coming to your aid."

"I was the one who fucked up!"

He flinched.

Panting, I turned away.

"You are clean. Go to your room and rest and I'll bring you sustenance."

I snatched a towel and wrapped it around me. I felt his eyes on me, felt his aching, lonely need.

I hated myself for hurting him but I left him and went back to the bedroom, lying down and staring up at the ceiling. Time stretched out into the heavy beat of my heart. There was a spider web on the right corner of my ceiling, a crack near the window.

Jaden's tentative knock made me jump.

He carried a Styrofoam carton that smelt warm and spicy and delicious. I sat up, my gaze riveted on the food. "Chickpea curry." He'd gone to my favourite Indian place.

"Eat, Mitchell." He offered it to me like tribute to a moody god.

I snatched it from him, opening it and taking the recycle-friendly wooden fork. Then I saw he was also staring at the food. "You haven't eaten much either."

"I have eaten nothing."

"*Nothing?*"

He stared at me and I saw the dark rings under his eyes, how wasted and thin he looked.

"Sit down on the bed." When he didn't move I snapped my fingers. "Sit!"

"Mitchell, the meal is for you."

"Fuck that, we'll share."

He sat down carefully as if afraid I'd get angry at him and send him away. Shame burned me. Jesus, how much of a fuck had I been? He was so vulnerable. I handed him the extra fork and we both dug in. He made a wildly enthusiastic sound I hadn't heard since we'd had sex. "Mitchell, this!"

"Yeah, it's something." I had to smile at the way he made a pig of himself. When he noticed, he gave me a guilty look, but I shook my head. "Fuel up." I pushed the remaining food to him. One thing about skipping meals for days on end, my stomach had shrunk so I was easily satisfied.

Jaden fell on the rest like the starving alien-human hybrid he was. He kept making those sexy moaning sounds and licking his lips until I was worked up again. Damn, I wanted to play human sushi plate one night and see where that took us.

His eyes were heavy-lidded with satisfaction when he was finished. He looked at me and made a soft, crooning sound, as if he were willing a sparrow from a branch. I curled up against him, safe, putting a leg over his, holding him possessively.

"Sleep," he said, his voice deep and soothing.

"If you stay, Jaden, are you going to give poetry slams in that voice?" I asked him drowsily. "Because you'd have a very appreciative audience even if your prose sucks."

Jaden tensed. "You wish for me to…stay?"

"Does it matter?"

His voice was so soft I almost didn't hear him. "Yes."

"I want you to stay, yeah." I squeezed my eyes shut. I didn't need to tell him I meant forever.

"But Mitchell…"

"Yeah?"

"I don't think I can write poetry."

I laughed. "That's okay. Neither can I. We'll find something else for you to do…if you want."

"We must deal with our opponent first." Jaden's voice was dark and primal. I felt an answering hunger for vengeance in my own heart.

"And get EZ back."

"Yes." His narrowed gaze promised me that. No matter what. "Sleep and you will think of a way. You are very clever, Mitchell. Let yourself only rest…"

Cuddled against his chest, I ran a hand over the flat planes, seeing the words inked into his skin. I wanted to kiss each letter. "Yeah, I guess…" I mumbled. "I just don't want that dream again."

"I will give you another," Jaden said.

"Wha—"

The last thing I saw was his hand moving over my face.

This dream wasn't like the one that had returned over and over again all week.

For one thing, there was music. I frowned, trying to figure out if it was a scale in A minor or C. Then I was walking on campus. It was a beautiful spring night when the stars above were a glittering carpet I couldn't help but pause and stare at, wondering… As I did, mist swelled up from the ground, surrounding me in a warm haze.

I wasn't frightened, but felt a sense of familiarity…and anticipation.

I knew it was my unusual lover and one of the games we liked to play.

The drum beats picked up tempo, a voluptuous rhythm that made me aware of my own sexuality. For years I'd stuffed my desires inside myself like a genie down a bottle.

I saw him standing on the path ahead of me. Even though it wasn't deserted, none of the other students who moved like shadows past us saw him and his bizarre attire. He was dressed in a shiny silver turtle neck and matching pants. He was holding a black ray gun. He was also smirking.

"Come with me, Earthling," he ordered in a husky voice that was Jaden trying to sound diabolical. It was about as threatening as a golden retriever's growl.

I stifled a laugh as he took my arm, leading me onto the grass where an equally gaudy silver flying saucer waited. I noticed the rotating coloured lights in the windows. It looked more like a disco saucer than a flying one.

"I'm going to use you for my experiments," he said and patted my ass as the saucer's door obediently slid open and I stepped inside at an imperious wave of his gun.

Once the door slid shut behind us, I wanted to jump him. I loved the over-the-top costume and the wicked sparkle in his eyes. I loved…him.

Jaden, however, kept up the impassive front, gesturing with an arrogant nod that I was to enter a circular room that held a clichéd metal table and instruments. I lay down on it without argument, my blood beating heavy in my cock as he shackled my ankles and wrists and then coolly snipped off my clothing.

Lying naked under his critical gaze I couldn't help arching my body wantonly, begging for his touch.

He caught my aching cock in one silver gloved hand and squeezed firmly. "Stop."

Breathing heavily, I nodded. I was his to do with what he wanted.

Satisfied, he put aside his ray gun and removed his heavy gloves, replacing them with plastic ones he snapped on. I moaned when he tapped his fingers against my thigh, opening my legs wider at his silent prompt.

He held my gaze as he grasped my balls, squeezing them and manipulating them as I panted. He gave them an exasperated glance and pressed a button so a small drawer rose from the table. After a moment of sorting through it, he chose a silver bottle, pouring the contents over my balls and around my erection.

I felt a slight burn and a curl of steam rose. Holy shit! The liquid had dissolved away my pubic hair, so now I was silky smooth. Jaden stroked my newly bared skin with approval.

He began to examine me, the skin between my toes, my inner elbow, behind my ears, all punctuated with harsh pinches to my nipples. He didn't touch my straining prick, which was oozing pre-cum shamelessly.

He removed a long needle device and, as I tensed, he slathered it with clear gel before inserting it into my anus. Once inside, the thing expanded and made a whirring sound. It drilled deeper inside me as he watched expressionlessly until it forced itself past the rings of muscle.

"Oh!" I couldn't help but gasp as it began to work on me, stimulating me so I could do nothing but lie there helpless, my body shuddering from the intensity of my arousal.

Jaden slapped my cock disdainfully. "Behave."

"Please..."

He ignored my plea and reached for a heavy silver clip, snapping it around my prick. Immediately it encased my organ, keeping me from release.

"Jaden!"

He raised his brows at me. "I have work."

"Doesn't it excite you at all to see me like this?" I asked.

"You are a very primitive life form. Easily moved."

"I want to suck you," I demanded. "Don't you want to see how primitive I can be?"

He regarded me for a few minutes while my body strained. I felt as if the very air moving against me could make me come, but he had all the control. I would come only when he permitted it.

"You are that eager, that in need?"

"Yes..." I whispered, knowing that I was tempting him despite his cold mask. "Haven't you ever wanted to take a pet?"

"You are offering to become my pet?" Steel glinted in his eyes.

"Yes."

"We shall see."

He pressed another button and the table moved, shifting me so I was suddenly on my hands and knees, facing him. He stepped into a U-shaped cubical and his hand slid down the silver front of his pants.

I licked my lips, seeing he was not unmoved by my performance.

"You wish to be my pet?" he asked me again in a 'prove-it-to-me' tone.

He opened his pants, revealing his beautiful cock, long and hard and brushing against my lips. Before I could arch forward to take more of him, metal looped around my neck, holding my head immobile.

His eyes were heavy lidded as he pressed his penis against my lips. "No, you can't move. You can only hold still while I use your mouth."

He teased me, rubbing his erection against my lips as he paused to take a readout of my body. I could not hurry him, he seemed almost unaffected. Finally, he thrust into my mouth.

I whimpered, crazed for the taste of him, crazed to come.

He ignored my discomfort, rutting steadily while I could do nothing but take him, over and over. He paused every now and then, studying the constantly updating graph of our bodies.

Finally his gloved hands tangled in my hair and he held onto my head as he thrust deeply, spilling inside me with a groan.

I swallowed, sucking strongly so I could please him.

He grunted as he pulled out, immediately turning back to his scientific analysis as I quivered, on edge.

When he looked at me again, he gave me an affectionate ruffle of my hair. "You are a sufficient pet."

I felt something cold and metal against my neck and then hot pain. He'd marked me somehow.

"You really need relief, don't you?" His tone was indulgent. He reached down and removed the heavy crushing clip from around my cock and I moaned as I jetted obediently into his hand with the force of my release, spattering the metal table.

"Good boy," he said. "I have examined you and labelled you; you are now my pet."

I shot up in my bed, chest heaving, but this time not from a nightmare. Across the room Jaden stared at me, his eyes glowing. He was playing soft tones on my

Hapi drum, which explained the source of the music in my dream.

"You…got into my head. Created that fantasy," I accused.

"I wanted to give you ease from your nightmares."

"I need *you* for that." I held out my hand and he didn't need a second invitation. He was across the room in a second, yanking me onto the floor with him. Before I could kiss him, he pushed me so I was leaning against the frame of my bed.

"Hold on," he ordered.

"Yes." I was so close. "God, yes."

Jaden ripped my jeans off like they were paper. He opened my cheeks and I felt his warm tongue caress me, sliding up and down my crease as I shivered. He kept this up as I shifted restlessly, hot and needy while he took charge of my cock, working me without mercy.

"Take me!" I wanted him in me, dominating me.

More tearing sounds and then I felt him against my opening, slick and huge.

I moaned as he penetrated me, his hands bruising my hips as he held me still. Sweat dampened the back of my neck and my hairline.

I couldn't hold back, widening my legs and tipping my backside up.

He thrust deep inside and my nails bit into the blankets. I contracted around him, coming hard. "So good…" I moaned.

I sagged against the bed, feeling his spend warm in my body, his hands stroking my back, his lips against my neck.

"My pet," he whispered.

Chapter Twelve

"No, no!" I gestured impatiently to Jaden. "Move it to the left. *The left!*"

He gave me an impassive look to let me know he was at the end of his patience. I ignored him, going over to the heavy equipment he'd lugged around easily in my lab and began to assemble everything I'd need.

"Do you need anything else moved?" His tone added *your highness.*

I nearly laughed. Jaden was finally using sarcasm after two weeks cooped up with me. He was truly becoming human.

"No. I want you to go out and get some food," I ordered curtly. "This experiment has to work in freeing EZ." I looked at my friend, who was still locked in her unearthly sleep, her face as serene as the statue of Quan Yin she kept in her apartment.

"I have been sending in her college assignments as you asked," Jaden said.

I couldn't be responsible for EZ falling behind. Jaden and I had been sharing the work. He actually seemed to be getting into it. If he managed to stick around would he change Jaden's major into women's studies?

"I don't like to leave you alone." Jaden paused to check on EZ. My throat tightened because her skin was so pale. She looked like a perfectly preserved corpse.

"We've been over this. You said it will take our opponent some time to regenerate. Now, if you don't mind, I have work to do..."

Hurt moved over his face, but I didn't soften. This was what it was like to live with a scientist. Sometimes I'd barely remember I shared a house with someone, never mind to shower or eat.

"I won't be long," he sighed. "Chickpea curry again?"

I nodded and instantly felt the absence of him in my house. He moved inhumanly quickly so I couldn't delude myself he was just my cute boyfriend. I still had no idea how we'd reconcile things if we could deal with the problem of Mr X.

No time to brood about Jaden. I picked up the cables I'd brought from the garage and began spreading them out carefully. I knelt, placing the last one beside EZ's capsule.

I felt a change in the room temperature.

I looked up, seeing Mason standing in the door of my lab.

"You're wasting your time trying to wake her," he said pleasantly. "It would take all of Jaden's power to do it and he'd never reduce himself so much for a human."

I swallowed. "My time to waste."

"Not for long." He was beside me in a heartbeat, hefting me by my T-shirt. "I should have dated you. If

I'd known how badly you wanted sexual release, it would have been easy to get close to you."

I spat in his face.

He slapped me. It was hard enough to send me crashing into the table holding EZ's capsule. I gripped the edge so I didn't fall on my ass. I could feel my face swelling from the force of his blow.

He cocked a brow. "I think I want to hurt you. I want that quite a lot. Interesting."

"You can hurt me all you want, but don't touch my friend," I growled. "You don't touch her."

"It would hurt you, if I killed her." He looked at EZ.

I rushed him. He caught my hand, crushing it in his grip. The bones broke like a brittle fan. I couldn't keep from screaming—

"Don't you…touch her!"

He dragged me to the capsule by the hair. Panting, I struggled but he was too strong, too fucking strong.

"Jaden will stop you!"

"Him." He smiled. "He was much weaker than I'd anticipated. He got in a few blows that would be worrisome if I didn't have just a human to contend with, but I ended him on my way to visit you. Bye-bye, boyfriend."

My eyes stung. "No," I whispered.

He reached out and laid his palm on EZ's living tomb. Blue light sizzled, blossoming into red and orange and sparking into fireworks with Mason at the heart.

"What?" He shoved me to my knees. "You are…unworthy."

The blast threw me across the room.

"Mitch. *Mitch-ell.*"

I opened my eyes. Pink. Brown. Annoyed. My vision coalesced into EZ glaring at me.

"Oh, Jesus. Get something on, will you?" I groaned.

"Like I dream of you seeing me naked." Her eyes filled.

"Goddamnit, EZ. *Goddamnit!*" I crushed her into a hug, breathing in her scent, feeling that familiar crackle of vitality that was my best friend.

"Close your eyes—"

"Please..."

"*Now.*"

"All right. Fuck, I forgot how bossy you are."

She snapped her fingers and I knew what she wanted; I shrugged out of my torn T-shirt and handed it to her. "There you go, m'lady. Anything else from your humble worm of a servant?"

"Who taught you to be so sarcastic?"

"You did."

I opened one eye to see her grinning. "Good job!"

"Yeah." My voice was husky. "I have to check on Jaden..."

"No need." His voice was very deep as he took my mangled hand in his. Energy tingled, but it still hurt as the bones reknitted. I took deep, yogic breaths, but it didn't do a damn thing for the pain.

"What did you do?" EZ asked, looking around my scorched laboratory. "Jesus, Mitchell, it looks worse than one of Mallory's crashed car sculptures in here."

"Simple jumper cables and my car's battery." I shrugged. "Sometimes the most basic science works the best. We channelled Mason's energy into restarting you."

EZ laughed but then sobered as we watched Jaden kneel next to Mason's body. "Is he, um?"

"He is alive," Jaden said and I felt a giant wave of relief. I hadn't liked the risk to Mason but it had been the only way to free him and EZ.

Jaden's face tightened as he pressed his palm to the centre of Mason's chest.

"Why didn't Mr X fight Jaden instead of wrecking your lab?" EZ asked. "I'd figure he would expect a big showdown."

"We gave him one. He wouldn't have fallen for our trick if he'd thought Jaden hadn't tried to take him on and failed."

"I did not like throwing my fight!" Jaden growled. "I could have defeated him."

I sighed. This was what Jaden and I had fought about the most when we'd come up with the plan.

"I'm sure you put on a good show before you let him defeat you." I swallowed because I hadn't known if he'd come out of it unhurt.

"Aw, you put aside your masculine pride for me." EZ got up to go to Jaden and kiss his cheek.

"Yes, for you. Our enemy had to believe we were not a threat."

Mason sat up, rubbing his head. He gave us a blank look. Oh, shit. Jaden had said there would not be much of his personality left after he'd been possessed so long.

"Hey, I know you," Mason said, gaze running over EZ. "Yoga chick. Nice pegs, girl."

"Jerk," EZ muttered, then glared at Jaden. "I thought you were fixing him! You couldn't add sensitivity?"

Epilogue

"God, that was amazing!" I huffed, falling back on the yoga mat in my lab where Jaden's sweaty body covered mine. He hadn't made a sound for a while. "Hey, you all right?"

"You are a constant drain on my energy matrix," he groaned.

I grinned. I was getting very fond of Jaden's energy matrix. "Yeah, I am, aren't I? Did we really go to Bora Bora this time?"

"I translocated us there," Jaden said. "You said you wanted to make love on a beach."

"Yeah. Except I think I've got sand in my butt."

"I will look." Jaden's eyes filled with sparks as he sat up to turn me over.

"No! If you do that, you'll be late for class."

He stroked my ass and I thought maybe his being late wouldn't be such a bad thing. "I will take away the residue of sand."

"Uh-huh."

"With my tongue."

"Oh, Jesus…"

He turned me over onto my stomach and knelt between my thighs. I felt his warm palms on my cheeks before he opened them and began to lick me. Slowly. Oh yeah, he was definitely going to be late for class, not that it was that big a deal. Jaden was still dabbling in arts classes until he decided what his new major would be. So far he had no interest in poetry.

"You're missing Women and Politics," I grunted. "EZ will be pissed."

"Men are pigs."

I grinned. "She doesn't say that as often now that Mason has worn her down enough to go out with him."

"She calls him a pig often in yoga class. You would know if you ever attended."

Oh, what he could do with that tongue. My body shuddered under each impact of its lash. "He was a persistent bastard, you have to give him that." My toes curled, my nipples like aching star points.

And then Jaden entered my spirit, gentle as the waves on the beach where we'd made out recently. I felt his mind mesh confidently with mine. He curled around me like a dragon, huge and powerful, glowing gold in the darkness. *I wasn't alone.* Tears pricked my eyes at the shattering intimacy. How could I go back to never knowing someone the way I knew my unearthly lover? My thoughts drifted past like windy clouds and he knew them as he knew me.

But the spirit merging wasn't enough for us.

He lifted my hips and thrust inside me, grounding me inside my body again. I looked back, seeing those dark heated eyes, that beautiful face that had haunted me even before he'd crashed into my life.

"Don't leave." Jeez, pathetic much? But this thing with us was still so new. I didn't want him to ever leave me. I didn't give a damn about interstellar politics. I just wanted to keep my boyfriend.

"I am your protector forever," he gasped, face strained as he strove to please me. He surrounded me, his aura and his bigger body. I might as well have been bound and helpless under him. "Making love to you is like the true death." He was letting me know he was as helpless as I was because of how he felt about me.

"Jaden." He meshed his fingers with mine as I came, the soul bond a starburst. *"You will never be alone again, Mitchell."*

After, I held him, arms wrapped tight around him. "Next time I'll have to get some readings," I mumbled. "I forgot again."

"My scientist." He closed his eyes. "And I promised EZ I would film us."

"Jaden!"

He laughed even when I slugged him. "I must rest and restore myself. My human wears me out."

I planned to do that for a very, very long time.

About the Author

Jan Irving has worked in all kinds of creative fields, from painting silk to making porcelain ceramics, to interior design, but writing was always her passion.

She feels you can't fully understand characters until you follow their journey through a story world. Many kinds of worlds interest her, fantasy, historical, science fiction and suspense—but all have one thing in common, people finding a way to live together—in the most emotional and erotic fashion possible, of course!

Jan Irving loves to hear from readers. You can find her contact information, website details and author profile page at http://www.total-e-bound.com.

2537187R00144

Made in the USA
San Bernardino, CA
04 May 2013